DMITRI AND THE ONE-LEGGED LADY

Michael Pearce was raised in Anglo-Egyptian Sudan, where his fascination for language began. He later trained as a Russian interpreter but moved away from languages to follow an academic career, first as a lecturer in English and the History of Ideas, and then as an administrator. Michael Pearce now lives in London and is best known as the author of the award-winning *Mamur Zapt* books.

ALSO BY MICHAEL PEARCE

The Mamur Zapt Series

The Women of the Souk
The Mouth of the Crocodile
The Bride Box
The Mark of the Pasha
The Point in the Market
The Face in the Cemetery
A Cold Touch of Ice
Death of an Effendi
The Last Cut
The Fig Tree Murder
The Mingrelian Conspiracy
The Snake-Catcher's Daughter
The Mamur Zapt and the Camel of Destruction
The Mamur Zapt and the Spoils of Egypt
The Mamur Zapt and the Girl in the Nile
The Mamur Zapt and the Men Behind
The Mamur Zapt and the Donkey-Vous
The Mamur Zapt and the Night of the Dog
The Mamur Zapt and the Return of the Carpet

The Dmitri Kameron Series

Dmitri and the One-Legged Lady
Dmitri and the Milk-Drinkers

The Seymour of Special Branch Series

A Dead Man in Malta
A Dead Man in Naples
A Dead Man in Barcelona
A Dead Man in Tangier
A Dead Man in Athens
A Dead Man in Istanbul
A Dead Man in Trieste

MICHAEL PEARCE

DMITRI AND THE ONE-LEGGED LADY

HarperCollins*Publishers*

HarperCollins*Publishers* Ltd
1 London Bridge Street,
London SE1 9GF

www.harpercollins.co.uk

First published in Great Britain by
HarperCollins*Publishers* 1999

This paperback edition 2017
1

Copyright © Michael Pearce 1999

Michael Pearce asserts the moral right to
be identified as the author of this work

A catalogue record for this book is
available from the British Library

ISBN: 978-0-00-825948-8

MIX
Paper from
responsible sources
FSC™ C007454

FSC is a non-profit international organisation established
to promote the responsible management of the world's forests.
Products carrying the FSC label are independently certified
to assure consumers that they come from forests that are managed
to meet the social, economic and ecological needs
of present and future generations.

Find out more about HarperCollins and the environment at
www.harpercollins.co.uk/green

1

'Try the Missing Persons Bureau,' said Dmitri coldly.

'Missing Persons?' said the Father Superior. 'What's that got to do with it?'

'You said someone was missing.'

'Not some *one*, some *thing*! The One-Legged Lady.' He looked incredulously at Dmitri. 'You've not heard of her? An icon.'

Dmitri knew, at least, what icons were. This was not surprising because nearly every house in Russia had one. It was usually situated in the opposite corner from the door so that you saw it as soon as you entered. The Church said that it was to remind you that you were forever under God's protection. Dmitri said that since this was Russia and Church and Tsar were hand in glove, it was to remind you that someone was always keeping an eye on you. Anyway, as you went in at the door, there it was opposite you, usually a face under a tin plate, of some saint or other, looking you accusingly in the eye. It always reminded Dmitri of his difficult grandfather.

'Not just *an* icon,' said the Father Superior with emphasis: '*the* icon. The Holy Icon of the One-Legged Lady of Kursk. The most famous icon in the province.'

He looked hopefully at Dmitri. Without luck. To Dmitri, icons and monasteries – and Father Superiors, for that matter – belonged to the Dark Ages.

'You'd better fill in a form,' he said unenthusiastically.

The Father Superior stood for a moment looking down at him. Then he said:

'Is there anyone more senior here? Boris Petrovich, for example?'

Boris Petrovich was the Procurator and Dmitri's boss.

'I'm afraid he's dining at the Governor's this evening.'

'Ah, yes,' said the Father Superior. 'I'm dining there myself.'

'This icon of yours,' said Dmitri, swiftly reviewing his position, 'it's gone missing, you say?'

'Stolen,' said the Father Superior. 'From the Monastery last night.'

Dmitri pulled a pad towards him.

'Value?'

'It is a holy object,' said the Father Superior.

'No value,' wrote Dmitri.

He had a niggling feeling, however, that something remained to be said.

'Famous, did you say? What is it famous for?'

'Performing miracles.'

'Oh, yes?'

Dmitri put down his pen.

'What sort of miracles?' he said sceptically.

'Well, it's transformed the finances of the Monastery for a start.'

This, admittedly, was the kind of miracle in which Dmitri could believe.

'How?'

'By inducing thousands of people to come and see her. Including,' said the Father Superior, 'Mrs Mitkin.'

Mrs Mitkin was the Governor's wife.

'Perhaps I had better take a look,' said Dmitri.

'Didn't I tell you,' said the Father Superior, 'that it performed miracles?'

The sun came up and turned the snow pink. The ice crystals began to sparkle. Far off towards the horizon there was another, larger, more continuous sparkle which became a flash of gold.

Gradually, the Monastery came into view. The flash came from a huge gold onion sitting on top of it. All around were subsidiary onions and scaly pineapples. They rose out of a

2

pink-and-blue striped roof, beneath which were walls so white that they seemed an extension of the snow. The gold was very newly golden and the pink and blue so fresh that it almost leaped off the roof at you. The Monastery, thought Dmitri, must have rich patrons.

There was a black smudge in front of the gates which resolved itself, as they approached, into a crowd of people. They held out their hands as the sleigh hissed past them into the Monastery yard.

'There are a lot of them,' said Dmitri.

'Who?' said the Father Superior, preoccupied.

'Beggars.'

'Pilgrims,' said the Father Superior, pained.

'Eyeing her all over!' said the monk.

'What?' said Dmitri, startled.

'You could tell he was no Christian. Didn't do his respects. Didn't even cross himself. Just stood there. Eyeing her all over, like I said. Disgusting!'

'Father Kiril, –'

'Most of them show a bit of respect. Not him! There he stands, eyeing her all over. Bold as brass! "Show a bit of respect!" I say to him. And do you know what he says? "Bugger off!" That's what he says.'

'Father Kiril, –'

Light began to dawn.

'This was an icon, was it?' said Dmitri.

'What did you think it was?'

'The One-Legged Lady?'

'Eyeing her all over –'

'He's always like this,' said the Father Superior despairingly.

The Chapel was dark except for a solitary lamp swinging down from overhead and the candles standing in front of the icons. The lamp turned in the draught whenever the door was opened and sent shadows chasing across the walls. Then it swung back again and they reassembled themselves. The candles fluttered and the faces beneath the metal plates seemed to alter their expressions but then the flames steadied

3

and they resumed their normal impassivity. The air was heavy with incense.

A wooden screen, corresponding to the rood-screen in old English churches, stretched right across the Chapel, separating off the chancel. This was the iconostasis. It was covered with icons. From time to time someone would come up, bow before one or another of the icons, cross themselves, mutter a prayer and then shuffle away.

It was from the iconostasis that the Holy Icon of the One-Legged Lady of Kursk had been taken. There was a big, raw gap almost in the centre of the screen. A length of chain dangled down on either side.

'We had it chained,' said the Father Superior, 'but they filed them through.'

Dmitri looked at the thick links.

'That would have taken some time,' he said.

'They had all night. There are no services between midnight and five.'

'The Chapel is left open?'

'Yes.' The Father Superior hesitated. 'Father Kiril likes to pray,' he said reluctantly.

'Did he pray last night?'

The Father Superior sighed.

'Yes,' he said. 'He was here all the time.'

'What?' said Father Kiril.

'Last night!' shouted Dmitri. 'The One-Legged Lady!'

He made motions desperately with his hands.

'Disgusting!' said the old man.

Dmitri looked despairingly at the Father Superior.

'It's no good,' said the Father Superior. 'We've tried everything. He can't hear a word!'

'Oh, yes, I can,' said Father Kiril unexpectedly.

'Except when he wants to,' amended the Father Superior.

Dmitri tried again.

'Last night –'

'What?' said Father Kiril.

The Father Superior preceded Dmitri through the door. As

4

Dmitri made to follow him, a monk, emerging suddenly out of the shadows, seized him by the arm.

'You don't want to listen to him,' he said, jerking a thumb in the direction of Father Kiril. 'He's past it!'

'I can see he has difficulties –'

'Difficulties!' The monk snarled contemptuously. 'He doesn't have difficulties: he's just past it. Addled. The milk in the bucket's gone sour.'

'Yes, well, –'

Dmitri tried to edge past. The monk gripped his arm more tightly.

'You don't want to listen to him!'

'Well, no, probably not, but –'

'But,' said the monk, nodding significantly, 'there are others who know more than they let on.'

'About the Icon?'

'Yes.'

The monk released his grip a fraction.

'Tell me,' he said. 'Why was it stolen?'

'I've been wondering that.'

'Well, why?'

Dmitri shrugged.

'Its value. I suppose.'

'Value? What sort of value has an icon got?'

'Spiritual, I suppose,' said Dmitri, remembering his exchange with the Father Superior slightly guiltily.

'Spiritual! Exactly! Well, who would want to steal a thing for its spiritual value?'

'I can't imagine that anyone –'

'Think!' insisted the monk. 'Think!'

'I am thinking. But –'

'Monks.'

'Monks? You're not suggesting that someone here in the Monastery –?'

'Not here.' The monk made an impatient gesture.

'Where, then?'

'There are plenty of other places that would like to get their hands on the One-Legged Lady.'

'Another monastery? But –?'

5

The monk cackled, released his grip and shot away.

'You ask Father Sergei,' he called back over his shoulder. 'He's one of those that know more than they let on!'

Why would anyone steal an icon? It was a question that Dmitri had been asking himself and which he put to the Father Superior as they were walking across the yard.

'Not for its intrinsic value,' said the Father Superior, 'its value strictly as an object, that is. It contains some silver, certainly, but it would hardly be worth anyone's while separating it out.'

'A collector, then?'

'I don't think a collector would be interested. It's too big. Huge! Six feet by four. And then the workmanship is a little crude. For my taste, that is. It's peasant work, really. I was saying as much to the Governor last night. Not that I would presume to set my taste against his. "There is that rumour that it's by the Master of Omsk," he said. "Yes, I know," I said. "But really –"'

'The Governor has quite a taste in these matters?'

'Oh, yes. He's got quite a good collection of his own. Nothing like Marputin's, of course, but pretty good.' He glanced sideways at Dmitri. 'You know Marputin?'

'No, I don't think I do.'

'Oh, I thought you might. He's down here quite often. Especially at the moment. He is a friend of the Mitkins'. I think,' said the Father Superior, 'that he would like to be more.'

'More?'

'Yes. He has his eye on the Mitkin daughter. Of course, he's much older than she is, but then, that doesn't matter much, does it, when there are other considerations?'

'What other considerations?'

'Well, the Mitkins are a good family. Poor nobility. Noble – on the mother's side, that is – but poor. Mitkin's often said to me that getting the Governorship was the saving of him. Marputin, on the other hand, is the son of a serf. Pots of money but no birth at all. So it suits everybody. Except Ludmilla, of course.'

'Ludmilla?'
'She's the daughter.'

The Father Superior was taking Dmitri to the Monastery gates.
'They're closed at night?'
'Always.'
'The problem as I see it,' said Dmitri 'was not so much taking the One-Legged Lady down – Father Kiril allowed for – as getting her out.'
The black smudge outside the gates had dissolved. A steady stream of pilgrims was crossing the yard and going into the main buildings. A smaller stream was heading for the Chapel: and there was another, countervailing stream going out through the gates.
'That may well have been the way she went,' said Dmitri.
'You don't think Father Sergei might have noticed,' asked the Father Superior, 'if someone had gone out carrying a six-feet by four-feet icon?'
'Father Sergei?' said Dmitri.
'He's in the gate-house,' said the Father Superior.

'Well, I don't know why he should say that,' said Father Sergei, surprised. 'Other than his normal dislike of me.'
'He spoke of another monastery.'
'Is he still harping on that?' Father Sergei shrugged. 'Well, it's true I came here from somewhere else. But that was fifteen years ago. You would have thought that after all these years –' He shrugged again. 'But that is Father Afanesi for you!'
'What monastery did you come from?'
'The Kaminski. It's near Tula.' Father Sergei smiled. 'Where the One-Legged Lady originally came from.'
'Perhaps that's something to do with it?'
'Well, it's true that they would like her back. It was a smart move of Father Grigori – he was Superior here at the time – to snap her up. But the Kaminski needed the money. She was paid for fair and square and, really, they've no cause for complaint. In any case, they'd hardly go to the length of stealing –'

*   *   *

7

The Father Superior had gone back to his room. Dmitri returned, cautiously – he had no wish to run into Father Kiril or Father Afanesi again – to the Chapel. He was looking again at the links when a carpenter came in and dumped a bag of tools down in front of the iconostasis.

'So she *has* gone!' he said, looking at the gap on the screen. 'Well, I'm not surprised. I reckon she upped and walked away in shock.'

'Why would she do that?'

'Because of what they were doing to her.'

'What were they doing to her?'

'Making money out of her. Making money left, right and centre. And I don't reckon she liked it. I mean, it wasn't what she was used to, was it? I mean, up in Tula it was the other way round. She was on the side of the poor, then, wasn't she? Well, I tell you this, Barin, she's not been on the side of the poor down here. She's been on the side of the bleeding rich!'

'The pilgrims don't look very rich to me,' said Dmitri.

'Not the pilgrims, although some of them have got more than they let on. No, the Monastery! See, everyone who comes puts a kopeck or two into the box and if you've got lots and lots of people coming, in the end it adds up to lots and lots of kopecks. And it doesn't go back to the poor, either. Do you know what it goes on? That roof. Now, I'm all for a lick of paint. I think it freshens things up; but the amount that's gone on that roof! And you don't have to go all the way to Tula, either, to find people who could have done with some of that.'

The bottom of the Icon had rested on a thick ledge which at one end had come away from the iconostasis.

'Now there was no need to do that, was there?' grumbled the carpenter. 'They could have just lifted her down.'

He knelt down and began working.

'I can do it,' he said. 'There's no problem about that. But what it needs is a proper base. If I've told them that once, I've told them a thousand times. But will they do anything about it? No, not they!'

He sat back on his heels and looked up at Dmitri.

8

'Mean as flint, they are. Do you know what Nikita Pulov was telling me the other day?'

'Who's Nikita Pulov?'

'He's the carter. Comes in twice a week. Would come in more often if they'd have him. Well, do you know what he was saying? He was saying that the other day when he was here, his horse drops a turd, and the next moment one of the fathers is out there with his shovel. 'I want that for my garden,' he says. 'Your garden's four feet deep in snow!' says Nikita. It'll melt, won't it?' says the father. I tell you they're after the dung even before the horse shits it!'

'Yes, well, –' said Dmitri.

'Do you know what I reckon has happened to the Icon?'

'No?'

'I reckon they've sold it.'

'Sold it!'

'Yes. To fetch a rouble or two. For the Monastery.'

'But I thought you said it was making them a lot of money?'

'Yes, but she's been here a long time. There comes a time when you want something fresh. Now, what I reckon is that they've sold her and very soon they'll start saying: "Oh dear, the Old Lady's gone for good. We'll have to start looking around for something to go in her place." And all the time they'll have had their eye on something else, another icon maybe, or perhaps a holy relic, and they'll get it and put it in here, and the pilgrims will start flocking, and they'll say, "Ah, well, reckon it was for the best, after all." It's a business to them, you see, and that's the way it is with business. Now you and I, Your Honour, may think we know a thing or two about business, but, believe me, we're like newly hatched chicks compared with them. Sharp as knives and about as much feeling. They'll have been looking on her as a carter looks on a horse: get what you can out of her and then get rid of her. So that's what's happened, I reckon. They've gone and sold her. Either that,' said the carpenter with grim satisfaction, 'or she's seen it coming and bloody well walked out on them!'

*   *   *

9

'So what are your impressions?' asked the Father Superior, as they were walking across the yard to the sleigh.

'Oh, mixed,' said Dmitri. 'Mixed.'

'A monastery is like that,' said the Father Superior fondly.

One of the pilgrims, a large man in peasant shirt and peasant boots, accosted them.

'I don't like it, Father!' he said.

'Don't like what?'

'This business of the Icon. If you ask me, it's not accidental.'

'What do you mean, it's not accidental?'

'I reckon it's deliberate. Taking her away just when she's needed.'

'What *are* you talking about?'

'Well, I've come here all the way from Tula especially to ask her something and when I get here, she's not here!'

'You can ask some other icon, can't you? We've got plenty.'

'Ah, but she's a bit different from other icons, isn't she? She knows what it's all about. She did something for people, didn't she? When they were starving. Well, I come from Tula, and we couldn't half do with her now, I can tell you, because we're starving again!'

The Father Superior tried to push past.

'Try some other icon. Or stay here for a day or two. We hope to have her back soon.'

'I can't stay here. Not for long, anyway. I've got a wife and children at home. My wife's sick, otherwise she'd have come herself. "I can't go, Ivan," she said, "so you'll have to. I know it's not your way, but we've got to do something and I can't think of anything else." So I've come, even though it's not my way. Besides, I thought the Old Girl might listen to me, she knows how it is for people like me. And now I've got here, she isn't here!'

'We'll, I'm sorry about that,' said the Father Superior. 'We're doing all we can. This gentleman here –' he indicated

Dmitri – 'is from the Court House at Kursk and he's going to look into the matter.'

'Ah, but is he?' said the peasant.

'What do you mean?' said Dmitri. 'Am I?'

'Beg pardon, Your Honour, but you people stick together. It might not be worth your while to look too closely.'

'Why wouldn't it be worth my while?'

'Because they're all in it together, Tsar, Church, Governor, all of them!'

'You watch your words, my man!' warned the Father Superior.

'They're not just my words, they're what everyone is saying.'

The Father Superior turned on him.

'Enough of that sort of talk! You go and find a Father and tell him I told you to have a few words with him!'

'Well, I will: but that's not going to bring me bread, is it?'

'What you need is not bread but straightening out!'

Dmitri had an unusual feeling as the sleigh approached Kursk; he felt that he was returning to civilization. This was not how he usually felt about Kursk. Dmitri was all for the bright lights of St Petersburg; and light of any sort, in his view, had yet to reach Kursk. Nevertheless, as the sleigh drew up in front of the Court House, he felt a twinge of, well, not quite affection for the city, more the feeling that a sailor has when after long months he returns to the land. Kursk, though on the very edge, was at least on land; whereas the Monastery was very definitely at sea.

'Oh, that icon business,' said the Procurator dismissively when Dmitri went in to see him. 'I wouldn't spend too much time on that if I were you.'

Which accorded pretty well with Dmitri's own intentions.

Boris Petrovich pushed a pile of papers towards him.

'These have just come in,' he said. 'Will you take a look at them? I am going out to lunch.'

The Procurator was always going out to lunch.

'In our position,' he told Dmitri, 'it is important to keep a finger on the social pulse.'

Vera Samsonova, the junior doctor at the local hospital, said she knew what *that* meant and that if Boris Petrovich tried putting his finger on *her* pulse again, she'd stick a syringe in him.

To Dmitri's surprise, however, he himself was invited out to lunch. To his even greater surprise, the invitation came from the Governor, whom Dmitri had hitherto supposed to be entirely unaware of his existence.

'Mr Kameron?' said the tall dark girl standing beside him. 'What sort of a name is that?'

'Scottish,' said Dmitri. 'My great-great-grandfather came from Scotland.'

'But how romantic!' cried the girl.

'Kameron?' said the Governor's wife. 'Is that the Kamerons of Gorny Platok?'

'Why, yes!' said Dmitri, amazed that anyone had heard of the small farm where his grandfather presently resided. The estate had once been larger but successive generations of spendthrift Kamerons had sold off land until his grandfather had put his foot down and insisted that henceforth male Kamerons should work for a living.

'Then we have something in common,' said the Governor's wife, giving Dmitri her arm and leading the way into lunch. 'Our side of the family have always been gentlemen.'

'But Mr Kameron no longer lives on his estate, Mother,' said the tall dark girl. 'He is a lawyer.'

'Well one has to be something. I suppose.'

'And how do you find the law, Mr Kameron?' asked the dark girl.

'It is at an interesting stage in Russia at the moment, Miss Mitkin. It could go either forward or backward. Until recently, as I'm sure you know, the only law we had was what the Tsar decreed.'

'Well, isn't that enough?' said the Governor's wife.

'Not always. What if the Tsar himself does something wrong?'

'But is that likely?'

'Not the Tsar himself, perhaps; but what about those who serve him?'

'The Government, you mean?'

'Possibly.'

'Governors?' said the Governor.

'Well –'

'These are radical notions, Mr Kameron,' said the Governor heavily.

'Mr Kameron is, of course, very young,' said the Governor's wife.

'But in touch with the new tone of the times, don't you think?' said her daughter.

'Ah, the tone of the times!' said the Governor's wife, steering the conversation into safer channels.

After lunch the two women retired and the Governor led Dmitri into a pleasant room which seemed to serve as a second sitting room. Its walls were covered with icons.

'Quite nice, aren't they?' said the Governor, seeing, and mistaking, Dmitri's interest.

'And some of them are not without value. They're all domestic icons, of course. Not,' he smiled, 'like the Lady whose acquaintance you have recently been making.'

2

'Dmitri Alexandrovich,' said the Governor in a fatherly tone, '– a little more cognac? – are you religious?'

The question caught Dmitri off guard. The fact was that this was a tricky point in the Kameron family. For generations the Kamerons, as loyal servants of the Tsar, had been members of the Orthodox Russian Church. Then with Dmitri's grandfather the line had hiccuped. Awkward as always, he had announced that he had become a Freethinker, with the result that he had been dismissed from the Tsar's service. His son, awkward, too, and determined, as all male Kamerons, to quarrel with his father, had conversely announced his return to the faith; only the faith that he had elected to return to was that of his Scottish ancestors. Since, however, there were no Presbyterian churches in Russia at the time, the genuineness of his return had not been able to be tested and while the Tsar's officials were working this out he had been allowed to continue in the Tsar's service and had been still serving at the time of his unfortunately early death. All this had left Dmitri in some difficulty as to his own position.

'Well –'

'My advice,' said the Governor, '– another cognac? – is to leave unto God the things that are God's and unto man the things that are man's.'

'Seems reasonable,' said Dmitri.

'That is what it says in the Bible. Or more or less. And I have always found it a sound maxim to follow. At least as far as the Russian Church is concerned.'

'Good idea,' said Dmitri. The last cognac had left him rather blurred.

'I commend the principle to you as a good one to adopt. Especially in the case of the One-Legged Lady.'

'But that's just what has not happened!' cried Dmitri. 'Man has just walked in and helped himself to –'

'I was not speaking of others,' said the Governor, annoyed. 'I was speaking of you.'

The haze descended again.

'Of me? Oh, yes, well –'

'And of the One-Legged Lady.'

The One-Legged Lady? Who the hell was she? It sounded intriguing. He must look her up some time. But, wait a minute –

'The One-Legged Lady?'

'Is no business of yours. It will only lead to trouble. You mark my words, Dmitri Alexandrovich, I have a nose for such things. You keep right out of it. Assume a wisdom if you have it not. That's what the English poet, Shakespeare, says. Or more or less. Wise man, Shakespeare. What he doesn't know about the Russian Church isn't worth knowing. You keep right out of it. That's my advice, Dmitri Alexandrovich. Keep right out of it.'

He had invited a few friends round that evening to celebrate his promotion to Assistant Procurator. Unfortunately, their congratulations fell short of the whole-hearted.

'You've let them buy you off, Dmitri,' said Vera Samsonova, never one to shrink from telling other people the truth about themselves.

'The surprise is that you were prepared to let yourself go so cheaply,' said Igor Stepanovich.

Dmitri fired up.

'If you tried to sell yourself, you wouldn't get an offer!' he retorted.

It had been a hard decision on his return from Siberia whether to stay in state service or to try to pursue an independent career at the St Petersburg Bar.

'But to agree to work for them!' said Sonya reproachfully. 'After all they've done!'

Sonya had recently returned from Europe, where she had

drunk deep of the liberal notions that the little group of friends liked to meet regularly to discuss.

'And you've said!' put in Vera Samsonova.

'If you want to improve them,' said Dmitri, employing one of the arguments that Prince Dolgorukov had used to persuade him, 'the best way is from the inside.'

'If you want to improve your career,' said Vera Samsonova nastily, 'the best way is from the inside.'

The thought, it must be admitted, had crossed Dmitri's own mind. It was all very well for the others to tell him to abandon his career in the State Prosecution Service and work for the greater good of mankind. The trouble was that mankind was unlikely to pay him; and if you were a young lawyer struggling to make your way in Tsarist Russia of the eighteen nineties, that was quite a consideration.

It was not that he was against working for the greater good: it was just that he wanted to eat while he was doing it. So when Prince Dolgorukov had approached him after that little business of the massacre at Tiumen, he had been willing to lend at least a quarter of an ear.

'You will rise more quickly than most,' the Prince had assured him. 'A glittering career awaits you!'

Unfortunately, it appeared to await him at Kursk. Wasn't that sacrifice enough, thought Dmitri, bridling?

His friends sensed that perhaps they had gone too far.

'I am sure Dmitri will do his best,' said Sonya conciliatorily.

'Yes, but for whom?' said Vera Samsonova.

'I do think that's unkind, Vera,' said Sonya severely.

'Yes,' said Igor Stepanovich. 'It's not surprising if Dmitri gets outwitted by someone like Prince Dolgorukov.'

Dmitri bit back his reply. With Dmitri biting his tongue and Vera Samsonova biting hers, the rest of the evening passed off amicably.

Dmitri told them about the One-Legged Lady.

Why on earth, asked Vera, would anyone in their right senses want to steal an icon? And in particular the Holy Icon of the One-Legged Lady of Kursk?

'Because it is encrusted with diamonds,' said Igor Stepanovich.

'Because it has miraculous powers of healing,' said Sonya, who had clearly imbibed insufficiently of the sceptical currents of the West during her stay in Europe.

Vera frowned. Russian intellectual society was sharply divided between westernizers, who saw in Western liberalism the best hope for the salvation of Russian society, and slavophils, whose views were exactly opposite. The little group of friends were strongly westernizers.

The group fell to discussing the general problem posed by religion for the development in Russia of a truly modern society. Sonya claimed that there was no problem since even Europe was not perfect and what was needed was a marriage of the best of Russia, which was its deep spirituality, with the best of the West, which was its progressive ideas. Vera said that no such marriage was possible because the two were contradictory. And Dmitri, after his fifth glass of vodka, heard himself maintaining that what Russia needed was a Dissolution of the Monasteries on the Scottish model (he had never been quite clear about the difference between Scotland and England).

The consensus was that religion was one of the things that was holding Russia back. As for the One-Legged Lady, the general view – put most forcibly by Vera Samsonova – was that if some old relic that smacked of superstition had gone missing, then so much the better. And what a relatively enlightened person like Dmitri was doing trying to track it down, the group, with a return to its earlier doubts about the genuineness of his commitment to progress, simply failed to see.

Even if Dmitri had been minded to return to the Monastery, he would have been unable to, for the Procurator had bespoken the sleigh for the rest of the week for a round of social visits.

'But the One-Legged Lady –'

'That old icon?' said the Procurator offhandedly, looking up from his newspaper, 'I'd forget about it if I were you.'

'But –'

'In any case, I can't spare you, I'm afraid,' said the Procurator.

Dmitri was surprised. The Procurator had always been able to spare him before. Only too readily.

'Too much going on here.' The Procurator waved a vague hand.

Since the only work that Dmitri was aware of were the cases that the Procurator had passed on to him, he was even more surprised. They were all of the 'she-put-a-spell-on-my-cow' sort. One of the duties of the Procurator's office was to assess potential charges and decide if they merited further investigation. Dmitri had taken one look at these and decided that they did not.

The Procurator glanced at his watch and put the newspaper down.

'You're needed here,' he said in a voice that brooked no argument. 'I have to go out. I'm having lunch with Marputin.'

Dmitri shrugged his shoulders and settled down to reading the latest novel from St Petersburg. At lunch time, feeling the need for a breath of fresh air, he went out for a walk and in the main street he met Ludmilla Mitkin. She was dressed in Cossack boots, a long fur coat and a small astrakhan hat and looked absolutely ravishing: a considerable improvement, thought Dmitri, on what usually walked down the main street in Kursk.

'Hello,' she said, 'would you like to give me some legal advice?'

Dmitri thought he would, and they turned into the park, where old women were sweeping the snow from the paths with brooms made of birch twigs. It had frozen hard the previous night after a partial thaw and the trees were heavy with icicles. They sparkled in the sun like chandeliers.

The last thing that Dmitri had expected was that she really would want legal advice. Unfortunately, she did.

'My mother's family,' she said, 'had an estate up in the north. It was where the family originally started and had been in our possession for nearly three hundred years. When the serfs were freed, we kept the house and a little land but agreed to pass most of it to the local peasants. It was the same kind of settlement as elsewhere. The Government lent them the money to pay for the land and they had to repay it over forty-nine years. Not surprisingly, most of them have been unable to keep up the repayments and now someone is going round offering to take over the repayments for them in return for the land. What I want to know is: is this legal?'

'In principle, yes; but a lot depends on who has title to the land. If the title was passed to individuals, then the man has every right to purchase it. Usually, however, it was not passed to individuals; ownership was vested in the village community as a whole. If that was the case then it would be much harder for the man to get his hands on it.'

'Why would it be harder?'

'Because everyone in the village would have to agree. And there is no way,' said Dmitri, 'that everyone in a village, not in a Russian village, at any rate, is going to agree.'

'Not even if they were all offered money? Lots of it?'

'The argument would be very persuasive. Even so, there would be someone who wouldn't agree. If only because he was holding out for more.'

'There is no legal obstacle, however?'

'Only that consent has to be found.'

Ludmilla looked cast down.

'I was hoping there would be,' she said.

'I'm afraid not. Why were you hoping?'

She hesitated.

'The person who is buying up the title has promised to return Yabloki Sad to the family.'

'Well, that's very nice,' said Dmitri.

'In return for something.'

'Oh, yes,' said Dmitri. 'What?'

'Me.'

When Dmitri got back to the Court House he found Maximov, the Chief of Police, waiting at the top of the steps. He rushed down to meet him.

'Dmitri Alexandrovich! Thank God you're here! Have you any idea where Boris Petrovich is?'

19

unch, I expect.'

ll he be back?'

, I would think.'

morrow!' moaned the Chief of Police. He seized Dmitri
oy the arm. 'You've no idea – I suppose you've no idea –
who he's having lunch with?'

'Marputin, I believe.'

'Marputin! Then he'll be at the Metropole. Sasha, you run
to the Metropole –'

'What's going on?' asked Dmitri.

'I need the sleigh. There's some trouble at the Monastery
about an icon –'

'Mind if I come along?' said Dmitri.

The smudge in front of the gates was bigger. From far off
across the snow Dmitri could see the huge crowd.

'I'm not going through that lot!' said the driver.

'Go round the back!' instructed Maximov.

'They always keep the gates locked!'

'They'll open them when they see us coming.'

'I hope they do!'

At the last moment the driver swung off the road and began
to head round the side of the Monastery. Some of the small
figures, guessing his intention, started running.

The driver whipped the horses.

They were round the back of the buildings now and could
see the rear gates. They remained obstinately closed.

A group of dark figures came blundering towards them
through the snow.

The gates suddenly swung open.

The sleigh dashed through.

Almost before they had passed the gates, they crashed
shut again.

'So what's all this about, then, Father?' asked Maximov.

'It's the One-Legged Lady. They don't like her being
missing.'

'Well, I don't suppose you like it, either.'

'They're blaming us.'

20

'Ridiculous!' snorted Maximov. 'They need a good kick up the ass, that's what!'

'There's someone whipping them up,' said the Father Superior.

'Oh, is there?' said Maximov.

He marched down to the gates.

'Now, lads,' he said through the bars, 'what's the trouble? We can't have this, you know, or else we'll have to get the Cossacks here. You don't want that, do you?'

'They've flogged off the Old Lady!' shouted someone from the back of the crowd.

'Nonsense! No one's flogged her off. Someone's nicked her, that's all.'

'Yes, and we know who it was!'

'No, you don't. You think you do, but you don't. Someone's been whispering a lot of nonsense in your ear.'

'She's missing, isn't she? That's not nonsense!'

'And we're looking for her,' said Maximov. 'That's not nonsense, either.'

'You're taking your time about it!'

'Well, it takes time.'

'Especially when you're not looking too hard!'

'Why are we listening to him?' said someone contemptuously.

'You'd do better to listen to me,' said Maximov, 'than to listen to some of the people you've been listening to!'

But the mood of the crowd was against him. He tried again but could hardly make his words heard in the general uproar.

'The Cossacks –'

'Bugger the Cossacks!'

'Let them come! We'll bloody show them!'

'He's always on about the Cossacks, this one! What about the Old Lady?'

'We'll find her, lads!' shouted Maximov desperately. 'Just give us time!'

'You've had three days! How much more do you want?'

'It takes time –'

'It'd take you time. It'd take you for ever!'

21

The crowd surged forwards against the bars. Maximov stepped back hurriedly.

'Listen, lads –'

'We don't want to listen to you. It's a waste of time.'

'He's in it with the others!'

A missile hit the gates, and then another. Several people caught hold of the bars and began to shake them.

'Lads –'

Maximov's eye fell suddenly on Dmitri.

'Lads!' he shouted with sudden inspiration. 'Lads, you've got it wrong. It's not me!'

'What do you mean, it's not you?'

'It's not me that's in charge of looking for the Old Lady.'

'Who is it, then?'

Maximov pointed at Dmitri.

'Him,' he said.

'Him! What does he know about it?'

'A bloody schoolboy!'

The shouting started again.

'Is that all they can manage to send us?' called out someone derisively. 'A fat-assed Chief of Police and a pretty Barin so wet behind the ears that he doesn't know his mother from his girl friend?'

There was a burst of laughter.

'Now that's just where you're wrong!' shouted Maximov. 'He may look green but he knows a thing or two. Have any of you heard of the Tiumen Massacre?'

'We've heard of Tiumen.'

Who hadn't heard of Tiumen? It was the great forwarding prison for convicts on their way to Siberia.

'Yes, but the Massacre?'

'I've heard of the Massacre,' said a voice from the back.

'Right, then. Well, this young Barin was the one who brought it out into the open.'

There was a sudden silence.

'Is that right?' someone asked Dmitri directly.

'Yes.'

There was another silence.

'Come on, lads,' said Maximov persuasively, 'it's either him

22

or the Cossacks. Now which is it to be? Leave it to him or have the Cossacks here?'

'We don't want the bloody Cossacks,' said someone.

'No,' said Maximov, 'I agree with you. We don't want the Cossacks. So are you going to leave it to him?'

He paused.

'We could give him a chance, I suppose,' said someone reluctantly.

'Give him a chance? Well, that's very wise of you. Now, look, lads. I want you all to go home and quieten down. Don't listen to anyone who tells you anything else. Give him a chance and if it doesn't work out, well –'

'And so, your Excellencies,' said Maximov virtuously, 'I decided I had to take action.'

'Quite right,' said the Governor.

Boris Petrovich nodded approvingly.

'If you don't jump on these things right away, I said to myself, they get out of hand.'

'Well, that's it.'

'You've got to stamp on them. At once!'

'Nip them in the bud.'

'While there's still time.'

'Exactly so, Your Honours. Oh, I know there are those who say that these things have got to be handled with kid gloves. But when you've had a bit of experience, you know that it doesn't do to hang around; you've got to go in hard!'

'Absolutely!' said the Governor.

'Good man!' murmured Boris Petrovich.

Maximov swelled.

'And so. Your Excellencies,' he said, 'as soon as I got back I sent for the Cossacks.'

'You what?' said Dmitri.

'Sent for the Cossacks.'

'The very thing!' said the Governor.

'No doubt about it,' said Boris Petrovich.

'You sent for the Cossacks?'

'I did.'

'But – but – you made a deal with them!'

'Deal?' said the Governor.

'Oh, I wouldn't say that!'

'But you did!' Dmitri insisted. 'You said that it was either the Cossacks or me and that you wouldn't run for the Cossacks if –'

'Pardon me, Your Honour, I don't think I actually said that. That's what they may have understood, Your Honour, but that's a different thing.'

'A very different thing!' said the Governor.

'In any case,' said Boris Petrovich, 'if there was an agreement, it was plainly made under duress and that certainly wouldn't hold up in a court of law. You're a lawyer yourself, Dmitri Alexandrovich. You must know that.'

'But it was deception!' cried Dmitri. 'A trick!'

'Justified, I would have thought,' said the Governor, 'when you've got a riot on your hands.'

'But –'

'What else was I to do, Your Excellencies? There was the mob hammering at the gates; missiles were being thrown –'

'Good heavens!'

'It was getting out of hand. Now I couldn't have that, could I? I'm a police officer –'

'And a very good one!'

'– I owe a duty to the Tsar –'

'Absolutely!'

'Not to say the Church –'

'The Church, too! Don't forget that, Dmitri Alexandrovich!'

'It's all very well for young people to criticise –'

'Young people! That's it!'

'– but when they've had as much experience as I have –'

'You did your duty, Maxim Maximovich!'

'No man could do more!'

'It was a question of *trust*,' said Dmitri. 'They weren't prepared to trust you. They only quietened down when you told them that it wasn't you who was in charge of the investigation but me!'

'Oh, now, come, Dmitri Alexandrovich!'

'This is vanity!'

'Your Excellencies –' Maximov spread his hands in appeal to the Governor's ceiling.

'Really, Dmitri Alexandrovich!'

'We all know how good you are, Dmitri Alexandrovich,' said Boris Petrovich spitefully, 'or, at least, how good you think you are –'

'Because of some trifling success you may have had in the past –'

'Which has been made far too much of –'

'But this is outrageous!'

'Dmitri Alexandrovich is, of course,' said Maximov smiling, 'very young, and in matters like this –'

'No, you can't have the sleigh,' said the Procurator, 'I have important visits to make.'

'Such as?'

'Lunch with Viktor Sharmansky, tea with Olga Vishinsky,' the Procurator ticked off on his fingers, 'lunch tomorrow with Sasha Radelsky, the next day with Irene Rodzhenitsy –'

'A theft has been reported,' said Dmitri doggedly. 'It is our duty to investigate it.'

'It is our duty to decide *whether* to investigate it,' corrected the Procurator.

'Are you saying that you have decided *not* to investigate it?'

'Oh, I wouldn't say that. I wouldn't say that at all!'

'Then –'

'It is simply a question of priorities. Naturally we shall investigate it. But with so much coming into the office –'

'*Nothing* is coming into the office!' said Dmitri. 'I insist on being allowed to investigate the theft of the Icon!'

'Dmitri Alexandrovich,' said the Procurator in a tired voice, 'there is a principle that I have always found helpful in such matters: leave unto God the things that are God's and unto man the things that are man's.'

'I have heard that before,' said Dmitri.

'I hope you have. It comes from the Bible. I think.'

'It comes from the Governor,' said Dmitri. 'I think. So you are not going to let me have the sleigh?'

'When the Cossacks go in,' said the Procurator, 'anyone else would be well advised to stay out!'

Dmitri sat in his office, first of all nursing his wrath, and secondly wondering how best he could pursue his inquiries while confined to Kursk. He was still nursing and still wondering when he heard the sleigh draw up outside. The door burst open and the Procurator rushed in.

'Dmitri Alexandrovich! You must come with me at once!'

He almost manhandled Dmitri into the sleigh.

'Where are we going?'

'To the Governor's.'

'What about?'

The Procurator seemed deep in thought. Suddenly he stirred.

'My advice, Dmitri Alexandrovich, is to say nothing!'

'Certainly. But –'

'And I will do the same.'

'But . . . what are we saying nothing about?'

The Procurator did not reply. He had sunk back into an agony of deep concentration.

'Why does the Governor want to see us?'

'It's not him,' said the Procurator.

'Who is it, then?'

'Volkov.'

3

Who on earth, thought Dmitri, was Volkov? As soon as he entered the Governor's room, however, and saw the blue tunic and the white gloves, he knew exactly who, or, rather, what, Volkov was. The Corps of Gendarmes was the specialist branch of the Ministry of the Interior which dealt with political offences. But what was a man like that doing here?

'Most gratifying,' the Governor was saying, 'most gratifying! But . . . a little surprising, also. Over a thing so small!'

'It may seem small,' said Volkov, bowing acknowledgement, 'but the Corps has learned to look behind things.'

'Yes, yes, I'm sure . . . but . . . a mere icon!'

'In itself it may be small. In what it stands for, however, in what it indicates, it may be much larger.'

'Well, yes. Yes, of course. No doubt about it. But . . . exactly what –?'

'Godlessness,' the Procurator cut in helpfully. 'The theft of a holy icon!' He shook his head. 'What is the nation coming to?'

'What indeed?' said the Governor, catching on. 'It is a sad state of affairs when –'

But Volkov seemed unmoved.

'Sacrilege?' said the Governor hopefully.

'A blow at the Church?' offered the Procurator.

There was a slight flicker – or was there? – on the impassive face.

'A blow at –?' the Procurator hesitated, searching around. 'Authority!' he cried, with sudden inspiration.

This time the flicker was definite.

27

'A blow at Authority!' cried the Procurator, confident now. 'At – at the Tsar himself!'

'The Tsar himself!' echoed the Governor in appalled tones.

Volkov gave an almost imperceptible nod.

'Or just a simple theft?' said Dmitri.

The cold eyes dwelled on him for a moment, dwelled and then dismissed him as an insect.

'Do peasants normally riot about simple thefts?' asked Volkov.

'Riot?' said Dmitri. 'I don't think I would go so far as to call it that.'

'The Chief of Police has asked us to send in Cossacks to put it down.'

'He is mistaken,' said Dmitri.

The eyes turned back to him and rested.

'Mistaken?'

'The icon was very dear to them. All they were doing was protesting about the lack of progress on the case.'

'Yes,' said Volkov, 'the lack of progress.'

The Procurator swallowed.

'We have done all we could, Excellency –' he pleaded.

'A mere icon,' said the Governor, 'a simple theft!'

'Riot?' said Volkov. 'Missiles thrown at the police?'

'Maximov exaggerates,' said Dmitri. 'I was there.'

Volkov looked at him almost with interest.

'Ah, yes.' he said. 'It's in the report. The young Assistant Procurator who lost his head.'

'Did he say that?' demanded Dmitri hotly.

'Certainly his own feats loomed large in the report,' said Volkov with a wintry smile. 'But then, we have learned to look behind that also.'

'Did he say that he had done a deal with them?'

'Deal?'

'That if they would disperse and give me time to complete the investigation, he would not send for the Cossacks?'

'I don't believe in doing deals with peasants,' said Volkov. 'Especially rebellious ones. Do a deal with them on one thing and they expect you to do a deal on others.'

'Quite so!' said the Governor.

'Absolutely right!' said the Procurator, looking daggers at Dmitri.

'So you will be sending in the Cossacks?'

'Not yet,' said Volkov, looking at Dmitri with his wintry smile.

'A glass of vodka after your journey?' suggested the Father Superior.

'Tea,' said Volkov.

The Father Superior went over to the samovar, which stood in a corner of the refectory. It was basically a large urn with a vertical pipe up the middle in which wood was burned to keep the surrounding water at the boil. The teapot stood on top with the tea leaves already in it and a little water, to which boiling water was added from the samovar.

'Sugar?' said the Father Superior.

'Lemon,' said Volkov.

'Jam,' said Dmitri.

The Father Superior brought the glasses back to the table.

'The peasants, then,' said Vokov, 'are unusually pious in your area?'

'Pious?' said the Father Superior, startled. 'No, I don't think so.'

'And yet they riot about an icon?'

'I wouldn't say riot, exactly.'

'What would you say?'

'I would call it an expression of concern. Which got a little out of hand.'

'Out of hand. Yes. And why was that, do you think? Why were they so concerned?'

'Well, the Icon was very dear to them –'

'Aren't all icons dear to them? What is so special about this one?'

'Its associations, I suppose.'

'Ah, yes,' said Volkov, 'its associations.'

He swirled the lemon round in his glass and glanced towards the samovar. It was an old one, not made of metal as most of the new ones were, but of some special kind of china, at least on the outside, which was covered with little blue tiles.

'And what are its associations?'

'Well, it's associated with the relief of famine. At any rate, up in Tula, where it comes from.'

'Ah, yes,' said Volkov, 'Tula.'

'It's quite an interesting story, in fact. It begins in the last century with a lady conspicuous for her good works. Among them was the relief of famine. She had the habit, whenever there was a famine, of driving around the countryside distributing food. Well, you know how these things get magnified in the popular mind. After her death it was claimed that she had performed miracles. You know, turning stones into bread, or if not that, bad wheat into good. And there was sufficient authentication for the miracles for the Church to agree, after her death, to an icon being commissioned in her name. It was paid for by public subscription.'

'Public subscription?'

'Yes. Unusual, that, I know. But she was very popular, you see. And some of that popularity rubbed off on the Icon. Whenever there was famine in the area after that, the Icon was taken out and carried through the fields.'

'Why?' said Volkov.

The Father Superior looked at him in surprise.

'As a focus for their prayers. It was believed that in some way she was able to mediate for them. We are talking of the popular mind here. There was some confusion between the Icon and the original lady. Of course, from the Orthodox point of view –'

'Ah, yes,' said Volkov, 'the Orthodox point of view.'

'– all this is a little suspect. Theologically, that is. But in rural areas –'

'And was it a focus for anything else?' asked Volkov.

'Anything else?' said the Father Superior, staring.

'There was always a lot of peasant unrest around Tula.'

'I don't see –'

'Especially in time of famine. You say that the Icon was carried round the villages?'

'Well, yes, but –'

'Which rebelled at that time.'

'Yes, but —'

'This is just an icon!' said Dmitri.

'It is not what it *is*,' said Volkov patiently, 'but what it *means*. In the Corps of Gendarmes we learn to look behind things.'

They stood for some time in the Chapel watching the pilgrims coming in. They came in a steady stream. As one group was going out, another would be coming in. Each group would go up to the iconostasis, genuflect and stand for a moment, heads bowed, before an icon. Often, then, they would raise their heads and gaze at the icon, sometimes for several minutes, as if rapt.

'It is good to see them accepting the disciplines of the Holy Church,' said Volkov.

'Well, yes,' said the Father Superior, pleased.

'On the other hand it is worrying.'

'Worrying?' said the Father Superior.

'To see how much the icons mean to them.'

He was looking at the large space that had been occupied by the One-Legged Lady. Many of the pilgrims went straight up to it and behaved as if the icon was still there. They bent their heads, their lips moved in prayer and often they would gaze as if they could see it. Some even kissed the ground in front of it.

They went out into the courtyard. It was packed with pilgrims. As they came through the gates they divided into several streams. One headed straight for the Chapel, another, carrying packs, made for the dormitory. Yet another went to the kitchens.

'Where do they all come from?' asked Volkov.

'Oh, everywhere,' said the Father Superior. 'And not just the province, either.'

'Where do you come from, friend?'

Volkov asked one of the pilgrims, a tall, bearded, wasted man.

'Tula, brother,' said the man.

31

'Ah, Tula?' said Volkov. 'And why have you come down here?'

'To pray, brother. And to look for succour.'

'Succour?'

'It's been a bad year up there. The crops have failed again –'

'And you, friend?' he asked another man. 'Where do you come from?'

'Galich. It's near Tula –'

Dmitri detached himself and started making his way across the yard to the gate-house. On his way he passed a group of men squatting down, oblivious to the snow, their backs against a wall, talking. Among them was the big peasant who had accosted the Father Superior on Dmitri's first visit. The man looked up and saw him.

'Still here, then?' said Dmitri.

'Well, there's not much point in going back to Tula, is there? With me away, what food there is will go further.'

'They'll miss you, Ivan,' said one of the men squatting beside him.

'Do you think I don't know that? But at least if I'm here there's a chance I could do something. Suppose the Old Lady turns up? I'd be able to get on to her right away.'

'There'll be plenty of others doing that.'

'Yes, but I can't just sit at home doing nothing. I'm not made like that. I can't just sit there watching them fade away before my eyes!'

'You've got to practise patience, brother. God will provide.'

'Yes, but He's not provided yet, has He? And if He doesn't start doing it soon, it's going to be too late. Now, what I reckon is this: He's a loving God, isn't He, and if He knew about it, He'd do something about it. So it stands to reason He can't have heard about it, and that's very understandable because He's got the whole world to think about and it's easy to miss a few corners. But, you see, that's just where the Old Lady comes in. She'd be there, knock-knock-knocking on the door, nagging away all the time, just like my old woman, and in the end He'd just have to hear, wouldn't He? And what

I reckon is,' concluded the big peasant, 'that's why they've taken her away.'

'You've lost me, Ivan,' said someone beside him, who had been listening hard. 'If she's the one who could get through to Him, why would they want to take her away?'

'Because they don't want her to get through to Him.'

The whole group was listening.

'Why wouldn't they want that, Ivan?'

'Because they're mean bastards, that's why. And because this way they've got us where they want us: on our back with their thumbs on our wind-pipe!'

'They're not that bloody mean, are they?'

'They bloody are!'

'I don't reckon you ought to talk like that, Ivan,' said someone uneasily, seeing the blue tunic and while gloves coming across the yard.

'I'm not afraid of him!' said Ivan.

'No,' said someone who evidently knew the family, 'but you are afraid of Agafa, aren't you, and she'll be up your backside if she hears you've got yourself arrested just when she's sick and needs you!'

'She certainly will!' said a deep voice behind them. It was Father Sergei.

'And they're quite right: you're needed at home! So let's be off with you!'

He bent down and with surprising strength yanked the big peasant to his feet.

'I can't go empty-handed!' protested Ivan.

'Who's talking about going home empty-handed? You come with me to the kitchens and I'll get Father Osip to fill up a sack for you!'

He shepherded the big man dexterously away.

'Anyway,' muttered one of the men as they watched them go, 'I reckon you're up the creek, Ivan; about them taking the Old Girl, I mean. She'd be far too fly for them. I don't think they've got her at all. I reckon she's well on her way to Opona by now.'

'You men,' said Volkov, 'where do you come from?'

'Tula,' they said.

'Aren't there monasteries up there?'

'There's the Kaminski,' said someone.

'What's wrong with the Kaminski?' said Volkov. 'Why aren't you going there?'

'Because the Old Lady is down here,' said one of the men. 'Or should be.'

'She used to be up there,' another man said. 'But then she was brought here.'

'Why was that?'

'I don't know,' said the man. 'It seems daft to me. Tula is where she belongs.'

'If she was up there,' said another man, 'we wouldn't be down here. We'd be going to the Kaminski.'

'And what would you be doing with her?' said Volkov.

'Doing with her?' said the man, surprised. 'Nothing. We'd be praying to her, I suppose.'

'It's what she'd be doing for us,' said someone, 'not what we'd be doing with her.'

'And what would she be doing for you?'

'Putting a word in,' said one of the men.

'You see, Your Excellency,' someone explained, 'word's not getting through at the moment. Not up in Tula, I mean. God doesn't hear us. There's terrible famine in the province and –'

'The Tsar hears you,' asserted Volkov.

His listeners seemed unconvinced.

Dmitri followed Father Sergei and Ivan to the kitchen. The way was blocked by a massive farm cart. On top of the cart was a large square behind dressed in a faded red skirt. The behind heaved and a shower of cabbages descended into a wicker-work basket that a man was holding beside the cart. They hit the basket like blocks of ice, which they almost were, having been dug out of a snow-covered heap only that morning. The woman straightened and Dmitri saw that her hands and forearms were bare.

'Cold work, Mother,' he said

The woman looked down.

'Not if you keep busy,' she said. 'You must try it some time, young Barin!'

She roared with laughter and bent down into the cart again. Another shower of cabbages hit the basket.

'Is that about it?' said the man below.

He took the basket away into the kitchens and the woman climbed down on to the ground.

'Who are you, then?' she said to Dmitri. 'You don't look as if you belong here.'

'I'm from the Court House at Kursk,' said Dmitri.

'Oh, you're after the One-Legged Lady, are you? Well, you won't find her here. She'll be half way to Opona by now. Or else that daft old monk has got her tucked away somewhere and forgotten where he put her!'

The man came back, this time carrying a glass of tea.

'This'll warm you up, Grusha,' he said.

'It'd warm me up even more if it had a spot of something in it,' she said.

The man laughed and took the glass away.

'You're in here every week, are you?' said Dmitri.

'That's right.'

'Are there many other carts coming and going?'

'Not at this time of year. There's Nikita Pulov bringing logs but apart from that –' She thought, and shook her head. 'More in the summer, of course. Sometimes you can't get into the yard for them. Them and sleighs.'

'Do you ever get asked to take things out?' asked Dmitri.

The old woman looked at him shrewdly.

'I wonder what you're thinking of?' she said. Then she laughed. 'No such luck! If they'd asked me, I'd have jumped at it. You don't get much for cabbages, you know. Not from this mean lot!'

'Who's a mean lot?' said the man, returning. 'Does that mean you don't want this glass, then?'

The old woman grabbed it.

'That's better!'

'I'd hope so. I put two spots in that, Grusha!'

'You're all right,' she said. 'It's the fathers I'm talking about.'

35

'It's true they don't throw their money around,' the man acknowledged.

'Except when it comes to tarting the place up,' said Grusha, looking up at the onions sparkling in the sunlight.

Dmitri found Father Sergei and the big peasant in the kitchen holding a sack.

'Bread won't do,' the peasant was saying. 'It won't last.'

'I was thinking of grain.'

'Will he go along with that? He is a mean old skinflint.'

'He'll go along with it, all right. He's a country boy like yourself. Comes from Bushenko. He knows what grain means.'

'Well –'

Father Sergei looked up and saw Dmitri.

'You go on in there and ask him,' he said, giving the peasant a push. 'And then be on your way! Oh, and drop in at the gate-house on your way out. I've got a few things I'd like you to deliver. My people come from up there,' he explained to Dmitri.

Ivan ambled out through the door.

'Now,' said Father Sergei, turning to Dmitri. 'What can I do for you?'

'Vehicles,' said Dmitri. 'Going in and out. Especially out. Even more especially, on the day after the Icon was stolen.'

Dmitri went round to the back of the building, where he found a cart standing beside a log shed. The cart was empty except for a few odd bits of kindling and some wood shavings in the bottom but two or three oblong wooden frames, as for windows, were leaning against it.

A boy came out of the shed.

'Peter knocks them up for the mill,' he said, seeing Dmitri looking at the frames, 'and Nikita takes them back in his cart.'

'I'm looking for Nikita,' said Dmitri.

'They're in the Chapel,' said the boy. 'If you'd like to come with me, Barin –'

He took Dmitri through the shed. Logs, some birch, some

pine, were piled high to the ceiling. Drops of gum glistened on the pine like ice and the air was pungent with the smell of resin. At the far end of the shed was a carpenter's bench. They scuffed through shavings.

They went out of a door and then across a little closed in yard, and then along dark cold corridors until they emerged in the main yard not far from the door of the Chapel.

Dmitri went in with a group of pilgrims.

'Where's the Old Lady, then?' said one man as they went through the door into the darkness and the candle-light.

Someone pointed to the space left by the missing icon. The group went up to it and stood for a moment before it.

'This won't do,' one of them said.

Reluctantly, they divided up and went to the other icons.

'It's not the same,' grumbled one as they went out.

The door closed behind them and the shadows recomposed themselves.

'It's not healthy,' said a voice suddenly.

Dmitri turned. It was Volkov.

'What isn't?'

'This attachment.' He surveyed the wistful, candle-lit faces on the iconostasis. 'Maybe it's a good thing she's gone missing,' he said.

Dmitri had thought they were alone in the Chapel but then behind the iconostasis there was the shuffling of feet. A door opened and the carpenter and another man came through dragging a curious wooden structure behind them. They saw Volkov's uniform and froze.

'The carpenter,' said Dmitri. 'And you're Nikita?' he said to the other man.

'Your Honour,' managed the man, hardly able to speak.

'He's the carter,' said Dmitri, 'he brings logs in to the Monastery. And what do you take out?' he asked the man.

'Take out, Your Honour?'

'He doesn't take out anything,' said the carpenter.

'I saw some frames?'

'Oh, those. It's a bit of a sideline, Your Honour. When they've got a big job on. I sometimes help them out.'

37

'What's this?' said Dmitri, looking at the contraption they were supporting.

'It's for the Old Lady, Your Honour. When she gets back.'

'The Old Lady?' said Volkov. 'The Icon?'

'That's right, Your Honour. It's for when they want to carry her. You see, she's very big and heavy, and if you tried to lift her up on to your shoulders, so that everyone could get a good look at her, you'd never manage it. She'd be too much for you. So what I've done is build a frame, which makes it a bit easier. I've put a couple of long struts on the back so that those behind can take a bit of the weight –'

'One of the struts needs a bit of work on it,' said the carter, finding his voice. 'Otherwise we won't be able to carry her out at Easter.'

'Out?' said Volkov.

'Yes, Your Honour. In the Easter processions, we go round all the villages and –'

'Out?' said Volkov. 'You take her out?'

As they were leaving the Chapel, Father Kiril came towards them, eyes blazing.

'Keep them in chains, I say,' he said. 'Keep them in chains!'

'Oh, yes?'

'That's what you've got to do. Otherwise they're up to no end of tricks. Down in the field, I've seen them. At it!'

'Yes, well, –'

'They're all the same. Give them half a chance.' He nodded towards the space on the iconostasis. 'She's no different.'

'She?'

'They took the chains off her. That was their mistake. She's no different from any of the others. Take the chains off them and off they go. Down to the fields.'

'Ye-es,' said Volkov, edging away.

There was a sudden commotion at the gates. Old Grusha's cart, on its way out, had skidded. The wheels had slipped round and into a snowdrift and now the cart was trapped against one of the posts.

'It's those damned fools there!' Old Grusha was shouting, pointing at a group of pilgrims. 'They wouldn't get out of the way! You've got no more sense than the horse, you haven't! Do you think it can skip around like you can when it's pulling a bloody great wagon? You –'

'Grusha, Grusha!' chided Father Sergei, running out of the gate-house.

'I'll break their bloody necks!' shouted Grusha, jumping down.

One of the pilgrims caught her.

'Father –?' he looked at Father Sergei.

'Just get her out of the way!' said another of the pilgrims. 'We'll sort this out in a second.'

Father Sergei took hold of the still-raging Grusha and began to pull her towards the gate-house.

'Come on in here, Grusha, and warm up. There's a nice bit of a fire in the stove –'

Gradually, he got her to calm down.

'A spot of tea, Grusha, to warm the inside?'

'I'd prefer a spot of something else.'

'You've had that already!' said Father Sergei sternly.

'Me? Me? The horse, perhaps –'

Dmitri followed them into the gate-house. The old woman stopped, befuddled, in mid-shout, as the warmth hit her.

'Never happened to me before!' she said, bewildered.

'It happened last week,' said Father Sergei. 'And the week before!'

'That wasn't my fault! He should have waited.'

'You should have waited. And you shouldn't have sworn at him afterwards.'

'Who does he think he is? Just because he's the bloody Governor –'

Volkov was waiting for his lemon beside the samovar.

'Tea?' said the Father Superior over his shoulder, seeing Dmitri come in.

'Please.'

'Help yourself to jam.'

He dropped a slice of lemon into Volkov's glass.

'Thank you.' He tapped the samovar. 'It's a lovely old piece.'

'It is, isn't it? Eighteenth century.'

'It doesn't come from these parts?'

'No, indeed.'

He brought the glass over to where Volkov was sitting.

'I really think you're making too much of this,' he said. 'All over Russia icons are carried in procession at Easter.'

'But *this* icon!'

'I know you're worried about the associations –'

'You think I'm wrong?'

'Yes, I do. That is all in the past.'

'You think the past is dead?'

'This bit of the past, yes.'

'I don't. On the contrary,' said Volkov, 'I think it's very much alive.'

'Perhaps it is in Tula,' conceded the Father Superior after a slight pause, 'but down here –'

'They come down here.'

'But that is because the situation is exceptional.'

'It is exactly that,' said Volkov, 'that worries me.'

'Whatever may be the situation in Tula,' said the Father Superior determinedly, 'down here, I can assure you, there is no political unrest.'

'You've just had a riot,' Volkov pointed out.

'I wouldn't call it that, And, in any case, that was –'

'Exceptional?' suggested Volkov. 'Too?'

He pushed his glass away and stood up.

'In a way it doesn't matter,' he said, 'not now that the Icon has been stolen. Or, at least, it wouldn't if only –' he stopped and thought – 'if only we knew where it had gone.'

4

'But this is daft!' said Dmitri, looking round the room. The floor, the tables, chairs and every available surface was covered with an odd jumble of articles: boots, shoes, galoshes, old coats, worn blankets, used shirts, shabby furs, and odd lengths of material. 'They don't need clothes, they need food!'

'Food won't travel,' said Vera Samsonova, looking up from the floor, where she was assembling various items into a parcel.

'Send money, then!'

'This *is* money,' said Vera. 'They'll sell them or exchange them for food.'

'Anyway, we are sending money,' said Igor Stepanovich. 'We've opened a public subscription.'

'How much have you got?'

'We've only just started.'

'The point is, it's better than doing nothing,' said Sonya.

'Or going around with the Corps of Gendarmes harassing starving peasants!' Vera shot in.

They had taken over the drawing room in Sonya's parents' house. On the second day her mother had asked tentatively when they could hope to have it back.

'When the famine is over.' Sonya had said firmly.

'But how are you going to get it all down there?' asked Dmitri.

'Uncle Vlady will take it,' said Sonya.

Uncle Vlady must be the mild-looking man who had hesitantly stuck his head round the door.

'But then what?' asked Dmitri. 'How are you going to distribute it?'

'The Tula Zemstvo is organizing relief.' said Vera.

'And Uncle Vlady is on the Zemstvo,' said Sonya.

That was one of the things that Dmitri had against zemstvos. They were the local councils that the Government, in an absent-minded fit of democracy, had recently introduced. Not as democratically as all that: most zemstvo members were noblemen elected by noblemen. They tended to be people rather like, Dmitri suspected, Sonya's Uncle Vlady, chosen for their docility and likely ineffectiveness.

'All that Uncle Vlady's got to do is get it there,' said Sonya. 'Vera has got some friends on the Zemstvo and they'll do the rest.'

'At any rate they'll do something,' said Vera, 'which is more than anyone else is likely to do.'

'The monasteries –' began Dmitri.

Vera looked at him incredulously.

'The monasteries? Have you gone back to the Middle Ages or something, Dmitri? Look, this is the nineteenth century, very nearly the twentieth, in fact. The right thing is for local affairs to be handled by local government.'

'Local government?' said Dmitri, who took the view that if anything was more incompetent than central government it was likely to be local government.

'Yes,' said Vera, facing up to him.

'As it would be in England.'

'Or France,' said Sonya's brother, who had accompanied her on her recent foreign tour.

'I favour the German model, myself,' said Igor Stepanovich.

'Everywhere,' said Vera, 'except in Russia. Up till now. The zemstvos are Russia's last chance.'

'The zemstvos?' said Dmitri sceptically.

'If we can't get democracy going locally, we'll never get it going at the centre.'

'Ah, well, there I disagree –'

But this time, unusually, no one seemed eager to join in a general discussion. They were all busy packing their parcels.

'You can help, too, Dmitri,' said Sonya pointedly.

With as good a grace as he could muster, Dmitri sank to his knees and reached out for a pair of shoes.

'Not that,' said Vera Samsonova, looking down at him. 'We need you for something else.'

'Oh, yes?'

'You said we ought to be sending money. We've set up a public subscription but now we need people to go round soliciting contributions. And since you've started moving in such exalted circles –'

When Dmitri got to his office, he was surprised to find waiting for him the carpenter from the Monastery and a village priest.

'Bibitkin, Your Honour,' said the priest apologetically.

He was a tall, thin, awkward man, dressed in the usual dingy brown robe reaching down to the ground and with long hair falling over his shoulders.

'Bibitkin?'

He remembered now. It was one of those cases that he had looked at and decided weren't worth pursuing. Something about a mother-in-law, was it?

'I'm afraid I don't think there's a case there,' he said.

'Exactly what I said!' said the carpenter.

'But there's got to be! She's complained to the Bishop and he's suspended me from all duties!'

'This is in any case a matter for the Consistory Court,' said Dmitri. 'We don't handle things like that.'

'But I've been to them! I couldn't get anywhere. I didn't have enough money for all the officials!'

'I'm afraid, however –'

'The thing is,' the carpenter broke in, 'he needs a bit of advice. "You need to talk to someone who knows something about it," I said to him. "Now, why not try the young Barin," I said? "He's a reasonable sort of man and he would understand."'

'Yes, but I don't really deal with –'

'Oh, I know that. I wasn't thinking of anything too, well, official. What I thought was that if maybe he and you could get together over a drink –'

It drove Dmitri to despair sometimes. The average Russian peasant could never be brought to understand that there was such a thing as formal procedure, a proper way of doing things, laws, even, that were independent and objective and applied to everybody. He saw them as something to be wheedled round. It all came back, Dmitri decided, to the fact that in Russia the law was still commonly seen as the expression of someone's, the Tsar's, will.

'A drink, that's all,' pleaded the carpenter. 'Surely you won't say "No" to that?'

Weakening, Dmitri agreed to be taken to the *traktir*, where, as he had correctly supposed, he found himself buying the beer.

'It's my mother-in-law,' said the priest.

'Yes, well, I can't do much about that. You chose her, didn't you?'

'No,' said the priest 'I didn't have anything to do with it.'

'Oh, come on –'

'Truly, Your Honour. The Bishop decided that. You see, when a priest dies, there's his wife and children to be provided for. So when a new priest comes along, he has to take over the wife and family too. And that includes the mother-in-law.'

'You didn't have any choice in the matter?'

'Not if I wanted the living. Mind you, if I'd known then what I knew later –'

'She was a hard old bitch,' said the carpenter.

'She still is. You see, I agreed that if she went to her other son-in-law, I'd pay her three roubles a month. And once she'd got these, she demanded more!'

'Well, you couldn't could you?' said the carpenter.

'I didn't have it. So then she goes to the Bishop with some cock-and-bull story about me and Marta –'

'Marta is your wife?'

'No,' said the priest, 'she isn't.'

'The thing is,' said the carpenter, 'that while he's suspended he can't make any money. Not from baptisms or weddings or funerals, not even at the big feasts, and what with Easter coming up –'

'It bears hard,' said the priest. 'It bears hard.'

'Well, I'm sorry, but –'

'It puts a strain on a bloke,' said the carpenter.

'It does,' agreed the priest gratefully. 'It does.'

'So when a person comes to you with an offer –'

'It's hard to resist.'

'What offer was this?'

'To buy the icon. We've got a nice little icon in our church. Several icons, in fact, but he was only interested in this one.'

Dmitri suddenly understood that he was being told something.

'Who was it who came to you?'

'He's been around before.'

'He's always around,' said the carpenter.

'Interested in icons?'

'And paying ready cash.'

'Of course, I wouldn't have looked at it,' said the priest, 'if it hadn't been for my mother-in-law.'

'Yes,' said the Blagochini grimly. 'I know Bibitkin.'

The Blagochini was the priest charged with the responsibility of reporting to the Bishop on the local clergy's doings and misdoings: the Bishop's eyes and ears, according to the Blagochini; his spy, according to Bibitkin. He lived in a little village outside Kursk. Everything about the village was wooden. The houses were wooden, with little gardens fenced off with wooden rails; the well in the middle of the street had wooden buckets and a rough wooden roof; the church, wood, too, had a green wooden onion on top; the tavern had a long wooden hitching rail running along in front of it, on the other side of which men were lying in the snow like fallen timber.

'It was nothing to do with his mother-in-law or with his quarrel with the Bishop. He just needed money to spend on his drinking!'

'And so he sold the icon?'

'Regrettably,' said the Blagochini, 'he sold the icon. It was not his to sell, of course. It belongs to the Church. But that's hardly the point.'

'No, indeed. And yet –' Dmitri hesitated – 'he does not seem entirely vicious.'

'He's a likeable rogue, if that's what you mean. He's popular in the village. Or was until this.'

'I want to know about this man who came in and bought it from him.'

'We've heard of him before. He's been going about the province for some time inquiring after icons. But not usually as brazenly as this. To go up to a priest and simply offer –!'

'He must have known about Bibitkin.'

'Well, yes.'

'Known what he was like. And that he needed the cash.'

'Everyone knows about Bibitkin,' said the Blagochini bitterly.

'Around here they do. But it sounds as if this man doesn't come from round here. So how did he know?'

'Someone must have told him, I suppose.'

'Yes. He must have local contacts. Now, perhaps you can help me. You say you've heard of him before. Do you know of anyone who has actually seen him?'

'Well, yes,' said the Blagochini, 'I do.'

Another wooden village, three miles off across the snow, a distance which the Blagochini cheerfully contemplated covering on foot. Dmitri had not bargained for Polar expeditions and cursed Boris Petrovich for once again having annexed the sledge. As they set out, the Blagochini glanced at the sky, which had turned unpleasantly leaden.

'We'd better not stay too long,' he said.

Dmitri had no intention of staying a moment longer than he could help.

The village, when they got there, was even more devoted to wood than its neighbour. It was dominated by a huge saw-mill, from which wagons were continuously setting out into the forest that lay behind the town. Near the saw-mill were two or three houses which were rather larger than those in the rest of the village in that they had a second storey.

The Blagochini told him that they had been built for the mill's managers. Avdotya Feodorovna, the woman they had come to see, lived in one of these. Her husband had managed the mill many years before and when he had died, no one had had the heart to turn her out. The mill had simply built another house for the next manager. Wood, after all, was cheap here.

Avdotya Feodorovna was old and frail and nowadays hardly ever left her house, although she had once, as she was eager to point out to Dmitri, moved in the province's best circles. She had known Boris Petrovich when he was a young man and a newly-appointed Assistant Procurator, 'like yourself, Mr Kameron, only –' her eyes surveyed him critically – 'much smarter.' She had danced at the Governor's balls (that would have been about eighty years ago, Dmitri reckoned) and had helped the present Governor's wife sell cakes at a charity bazaar when the Mitkins had first come to the district. In more recent years she had had to confine her social activities to the local church.

'Where at least our priest doesn't sell the icons,' she said tartly.

It had been at the church that she had seen the man. She remembered the occasion well because it had occurred only a few days before Bibitkin's disgraceful action had rocked the congregations of the little churches of the villages scattered on that side of Kursk.

'To think what might have happened,' she said, rolling her eyes dramatically, 'if I had not come in at that moment!'

The church had been empty except for the man peering intently at one of the church's small collection of icons. He had, she said, jumped back – 'guiltily' – when he had heard her come in. But then had gone across to her and – mistaking her for one of the ladies who came in regularly to clean the church – complimented her on the meticulousness with which it was kept. He had, he said, been drawn into the church by its general air of peacefulness and then had been struck by the beauty of its icons. They were not particularly special, he had said – 'except in the eyes of God,' she had retorted – but had a certain charm. He had asked her if the church possessed perhaps, some more noted icons which, for safety's sake, it kept locked away. She had told him about the Holy Icon of Saint Seraphina and he had nodded as if he had heard of it but then had seemed to lose interest. The workmanship is a little heavy, don't you think?' he had said. Although she was sure it was no heavier than that of the icon he had been so anxious to buy from Bibitkin!

Dmitri asked her what the man had looked like.

'From the city,' she said.

'A gentleman?'

She hesitated.

'Not quite,' she said at last. 'Dressed like one. Well-spoken, well-groomed. A little chestnut beard, well-cut. Moustaches carefully trimmed. But –' she hesitated again, 'a little too carefully done, if you know what I mean.' She thought again. 'More like one of those men that work in the big shops of Saint Petersburg than like a real gentleman. Except – except for his hands.' She shook her head and laughed. 'You'd never see hands like those in a shop in Saint Petersburg. They were workman's hands. Big, rough, worn hands. No,' she said, laughing again, 'you wouldn't see hands like those in Saint Petersburg.'

Dmitri nodded. It tallied with the description he'd had from Bibitkin.

While they had been in the house, it had started to snow and now the flakes were falling steadily out of a sky that was heavy in all directions.

'I'll see if they've got a cart going in your direction,' said the Blagochini.

He disappeared into the saw-mill office and shortly after-wards re-emerged with the foreman.

'We've got one going over to Baluki, Your Excellency,' he said to Dmitri.

'That'll do.'

Baluki was only a mile or so outside the city. Even Dmitri could manage that.

'Nikita!' called the Foreman.

Out from a shed came the driver whom Dmitri had last seen at the Monastery helping the carpenter move the frame for the Old Lady.

'Your Honour!' he said, touching his cap to Dmitri in recognition.

'Nikita Pulov?'

'He'll soon get you there,' said the foreman.

The driver eyed the sky.

'The sooner, the better,' he said.

He took Dmitri through the saw-mill yard to where his cart was standing along with some others. Before climbing up into the seat, he rummaged in the back of the cart and produced some sacking, which he gave to Dmitri.

'You'll need that,' he said.

Dmitri wrapped it round his knees and turned up his collar. As the horse and cart headed out of the dirty, trodden snow of the yard into the pristine whiteness of the fields, the falling flakes covered the sacking within seconds.

'I'm taking you out of your way,' apologised Dmitri.

'No you're not. Baluki is where I live.'

The snow was falling heavily in thick flakes. Already there was no distinction between the track and the fields. Anything more than a few yards beyond them was blotted out by a dense veil of falling snow. How the carter could tell the way Dmitri could not think. He headed confidently on, however.

'What brings you here, then?' said the carter suddenly.

'Bibitkin. I thought I'd come over here to find out what it's all about.'

'You'll be doing well if you do that.'

They carried on for a little way in silence.

'Mind you,' said the carter, after a while, 'he's not as black as he's painted.'

'Bibitkin? Yes, but to sell an icon!'

'What's an icon?'

'Which wasn't even his!'

'I don't know about that, either,' said the carter, after some time. 'The icon belongs to the Church, doesn't it? And the Church belongs to us or so they say.'

While Dmitri was reflecting how to put right these legal, and logical, errors, the carter surprisingly, spoke again.

'There was a time,' he said, 'when it all belonged to the people. The churches, the monasteries, the land –' he made a wide, sweeping gesture – 'everything. And then they took

49

it away from them! The Tsar came along, and the boyars, and they took everything away. You didn't have monasteries then. You didn't need to. People led pure, simple lives. You didn't even need a church – much less a priest! The elders looked after it all. That's how it was. But then the Tsar came along, and the boyars, and they took it away and always after that there was rich men and poor men.'

'Well, yes,' said Dmitri, 'but –'

'Take my own village,' said the carter, 'Baluki. Oh, it's not much of a place now, I'll grant you that. But there was a time when all the land around it belonged to the *mir*, the village community. They parcelled it out each year for families to work. It didn't belong to them, it belonged to everybody. They just had the right to work it and benefit from it. But then rich men came along and they chipped at it and chipped at it, and now all the best land belongs to them. There isn't enough land now for everyone to work. So people have got to work out of the village. Why do you think I'm a carter? It's because my old man said to me, "Nikita," he said, "Nikita, you're going to have to go and do something else." "I'm not going to work for that bloody Monastery," I said. "All right, then," he said, "you'd better go and work for that bloody saw-mill!" And that's what I did. But it's not right. Because they've taken it all away from us, and now they're rich and we're poor. So what I say is,' the carter concluded, 'Bibitkin's not as wrong as he looks. And if that old bitch would only leave him alone –'

'What do you think of that?' asked the Procurator next morning, holding up a picture for Dmitri to see. It was of a large demon-like figure holding a shrinking girl in its clutches.

'Oh, gripping,' said Dmitri. 'Very.'

'Thought you'd like it,' said Boris Petrovich, pleased. He put the picture down on his desk. 'It's for my wife. It's her birthday next week. I always give her something like this.'

'A picture?'

'Something with tone. Tone,' said the Procurator, 'is very important in a profession like ours. One has to mix, you know, with the highest as well as the lowest. And the first thing they ask is: has he got tone? Is he the sort of man I could introduce to my wife? Or daughter.'

Dmitri's warning antennae began to react quickly. Daughter? Had the Procurator got a daughter? Was that the girl he'd seen him with last year? But she was only about fifteen! But that was last year and this year she would be – ·

'I'm not so sure about that, Boris Petrovich,' he said quickly, 'tone is one thing, I think, and taste is another. Now, tastes differ –'

But the Procurator wasn't listening. He was looking at his watch.

'I'm afraid I won't have time to do it myself,' he said. 'I'm off to lunch with Elena Vinogradskaya. Could you do it for me? Would you mind? Something simple. Elegant. Gold, perhaps. In colour, I mean. He'll know what to suggest.'

'Who –?'

'Tretchikov. The artist. He does framing, too. Would you ask him –? By next week, remember. Wednesday.'

'But its snowing!' said Dmitri.

'Cover it up. There's some paper in the office.'

'How about the sleigh?' asked Dmitri, who had had enough arctic navigation recently.

'The sleigh? But you've forgotten. I'm using it. To go to Vinogradskaya's –'

'She's only just along the road. You could –'

'In our position,' said the Procurator, pained, 'one needs to travel with tone.'

'It's shit!' said the artist. 'This kind of thing went out centuries ago. It's not worth framing.'

'That's what he wants. And he's prepared to pay for it.'

'Well, in that case –' The artist sighed. 'You don't feel like a drink?' he said hopefully.

They went across the road to a *traktir*.

'I'll have a vodka,' said the artist. 'And why don't you get a bottle while you're at it?'

He poured out two glasses, tossed his off in a mouthful and poured himself another.

'Do you know what's wrong with Russia?' he said.

'Yes,' said Dmitri. It was a country in which everyone expected you to buy them a drink. 'No?' he said.

'It's backward-looking. Take that picture of yours. It's a reproduction, of course, and a bad one at that. But when do you think the original was painted?'

'Well –'

'You'd think it was the last century, wouldn't you? Well, it wasn't. It was painted just three years ago. Wood-Demons! And we're nearly in the twentieth century. And yet people still buy the stuff!'

'Not me,' said Dmitri. 'Boris Petrovich.'

'Well, anyway. And yet you can't blame them. We artists are just as bad. The thing is, you see –'

He tossed off two more vodkas. The level in the bottle was beginning to descend alarmingly.

– 'as with everything else in Russia, there are two sides: the Westernizers and the Old Russia-ites. It's true that the Westernizers haven't got very far yet. I know what you're thinking. Where, you are going to say, are our Renoirs and Manets and Monets?'

He looked expectantly at Dmitri.

'Where are our Monets and Manets?' echoed Dmitri obediently. He was already beginning to realize that the artist was a man it was unwise to try to drink level with.

'They're on the way, that's the answer. We're coming. I could show you one or two little ateliers in St Petersburg – though, of course, you don't have to go to St Petersburg. I could show you one or two things *here*. In fact, why don't we go across to my studio now and –'

'Some other time, perhaps,' said Dmitri hastily.

'We could always go later, I suppose,' said the artist unwillingly. He seized the bottle and poured out two more drinks. 'Where was I?' he continued thickly.

'With the Westernizers.'

'Ah, yes. Well –'

'And the Easternizers,' said Dmitri helpfully. He was beginning to feel light-headed.

'Easternizers?'

'Wood-Demons and all that shit,' said Dmitri, giggling.

'Oh, them. Mind you, I've got nothing against the Wanderers.'

'Me neither,' said Dmitri. He giggled again. 'Who are they?'

'I'm all for reviving the traditional arts of the countryside.'

'Dead right!' said Dmitri enthusiastically.

'Icons are part of our Russian heritage.'

'Icons?' said Dmitri. For a moment the swirling mists cleared.

'They're all the fashion now. You'd be surprised how business is booming. The icon-makers are in clover.'

'People are buying them?'

'Oh, yes.'

There was something in the mist that Dmitri was desperately trying to get hold of.

'Stealing them?'

'Stealing them?' The artist stared at Dmitri. 'Well, maybe. I don't know.'

The mist lurched away again.

'Collecting them, anyway?'

'Oh, yes. The collectors are in with a vengeance.'

'What do they do with them?'

'Do with them? Put them on the wall, I suppose.'

'How would you know that somebody had got such and such an icon in his collection?'

'You wouldn't unless you looked. Of course, you hear from time to time when other people have looked, but –'

'There are no dealers who would know?'

'We don't have many dealers yet. Not for paintings, anyway. You have to go to Paris. That's where the big people go, the Morozovs and the Shchukins. If you want a Monet or a Manet –'

'Icons,' said Dmitri, 'what about icons?'

'There aren't any dealers as such. Not for icons. It's all too recent. People haven't got used to thinking of icons as art objects yet. There are one or two places in St Petersburg and Moscow that sell icons and do a bit of restoring and they might have an idea what icons there are about, but –'

He poured the last of the bottle into his glass.

'The thing is,' he said, 'there isn't really a market for art in Russia. Not for good art, anyway. Maybe it's just beginning. And I'm not saying that the Wanderers haven't done their bit. I'm all for going about the provinces taking art to the people. The question is, though, what art are you taking? If it's stuff like the Wood-Demon, well –'

He drained his glass and put it down.

'If you feed a Russian shit, he'll develop a taste for it, won't he?'

'Who's feeding Russians shit?' demanded the man at the next table.

The artist stood up and waved his arms excitedly.

'They all are! The Academy! The Schools –'

'I'm not being fed shit!' said the man, rising unsteadily to his feet and hurling his tankard in the artist's direction. The artist seized the bottle –

5

'What on earth have you been doing?' asked the Procurator in astonishment.

'Attempting to quell a riot,' said Dmitri.

'I think that sort of thing is best left to the police,' said Boris Petrovich.

'So do I,' said Dmitri.

The Procurator drummed his fingers on the table.

'I must ask you to avoid such incidents in future, Dmitri Alexandrovich. At least for the time of the election.'

'Election?'

'For the Zemstvo. I have,' said the Procurator, preening himself, 'been solicited to stand.'

'Who by?'

'His Excellency, the Governor.'

First Uncle Vlady: now Boris Petrovich.

'They're not all like that,' protested Vera Samsonova that evening when he told her about it. 'There are lots of new people coming on. Doctors, engineers, surveyors; practical people with a bit of sense.'

'Lawyers?'

'I wasn't including them. Too many of them are like Boris Petrovich. In any case, they're not going to change things, not the way the others are. They're too inclined to side with the authorities.'

'I don't know that any of them are likely to be that independent,' said Dmitri, 'not if they're being elected by the likes of the Governor.'

'Of course, the franchise is too narrow. It must be widened beyond the gentry. Even so, liberal, practical people are increasingly creeping on. Not here, perhaps, but certainly up in Tula.'

'Uncle Vlady?'

Vera made a gesture of impatience.

'There are others. The point is, the Zemstvo is there and we've got to use it. We mustn't leave it in the hands of people like Boris Petrovich.'

Dmitri was inclined to agree. That morning, though, when the Procurator had told him of his intention, he had accepted it as merely another of the many pointless things that Boris Petrovich occupied himself with.

'I am sure you will add lustre to the Zemstvo's deliberations,' he had said politely.

'Well, yes,' said Boris Petrovich, 'so I flatter myself. I shall bring a wider perspective to bear on the issues than many of the other members can . . . a practical analytical brain . . . experience . . . dare I say . . . wisdom?'

Dmitri thought not, but confined himself to saying that with the Governor's support the election should surely be a shoe-in.

Boris Petrovich, however, frowned.

'One would have thought so. But –'

'Surely he can count on the support of the gentry?'

'We-ell, yes, but – the fact is, Dmitri Alexandrovich, the Governor is not as popular as one would like. None of us is. I mean, no one who holds a position of authority. It is the price of responsibility. You have to take decisions, and when you do, there is always going to be someone who doesn't like them. And then, you know, Dmitri Alexandrovich, the mood of the country is changing – it is not enough to mend the roads. I mean, supposing there were any roads. People want more these days, hospitals, schools, things like that. It is no longer enough to, well, just let them appear. And the Governor has been criticised by some for a certain lack of commitment –'

'But you yourself, Boris Petrovich, are personally known to many of the electors. I mean, you're always going out to lunch – that, surely, must count for something?'

'One hopes so. One hopes so. But –' The Procurator shook

his head worriedly. 'I fear that they think of me as a man of intellect, purely. They think I lack feeling. The women, especially. There's a vogue these days, especially among the women, for sentimental feeling on public affairs, the poor, you know, all that sort of thing, and – well, you know me, Dmitri Alexandrovich, I'm hard-headed, and I fear it will count against me –'

The glimmering of an idea came to Dmitri.

'Boris Petrovich,' he said, 'you must show them otherwise.'

'Well, I would, but – I'm not a man who wears his heart on his sleeve, Dmitri Alexandrovich. I mean, I love my wife – look at the way I'm buying her a birthday present – but –'

Dmitri shook his head.

'It's got to be wider than that, Boris Petrovich.'

'Well yes, but –'

'I have an idea. There is a public subscription being got up locally to relieve famine –'

'Famine? I didn't know there was one.'

'Not here. Up in Tula.'

'Tula? Oh, that's all right.'

'Why don't you go round soliciting subscriptions? You could combine it with lunch.'

'You think so?'

'Ah, yes. And it would show that you have a heart as well as a head.'

'Why, yes, so it would. But, Dmitri Alexandrovich, don't you think –? Famine relief: isn't that a bit, well, radical?'

'It's up in Tula.'

'Well, yes, it does help if it's a long way away.'

'It makes you seem disinterested.'

'That's true. And there's another thing, too. If it was here, they might ask why I wasn't doing something about it anyway.'

'But if it's up in Tula –'

'And absolutely nothing to do with us –! Yes,' said the Procurator, with growing enthusiasm, 'absolutely nothing to do with us –'

* * *

Volkov called in on his way to the Governor's.

'Good heavens!' he said, when he saw Dmitri's face. 'What have you been doing?'

'Attempting to quell a riot,' said Dmitri.

'Another one?' said Volkov grimly.

He called in again later in the morning and announced that he was taking Dmitri with him to the Monastery.

'And you'd better come too,' he said to Boris Petrovich.

'But what about the office?' said the Procurator unhappily, mindful of his social engagements and uneasy anyway in the presence of Volkov.

'We'll only be away for a couple of days,' said Volkov.

His sleigh was big enough to accommodate the two of them, as well as the Chief of Police, whom they found sitting miserably in the back waiting for them. What Volkov was seeking to achieve with this galaxy of talent, Dmitri could not work out. He said nothing throughout the whole of the journey and after a few attempts at conversation Boris Petrovich sunk, like Maximov, into a slough of despond, brightening only, as they approached the Monastery, at the thought that at least the Father Superior kept a good table.

When they arrived, Volkov installed himself in the Father Superior's rooms and ordered the monks to be brought before him one by one. Maximov was sent on some special business to do with the pilgrims; and Dmitri headed for the door.

'Where are you going?' said Volkov.

'To carry on with my inquiries,' said Dmitri.

Volkov considered.

'I suppose it makes sense for us to cover separate things,' he conceded.

Boris Petrovich wavered uncertainly.

'I think I will review the general position,' he said.

He asked Dmitri to take him to the Chapel. The stream of pilgrims was still flowing unabated. They went up to the icon-ostasis, inclined before one or other of the icons, muttered a prayer and then, after some moments of reflection, shuffled on out again. As before, many of them went up to the space where the One-Legged Lady had hung and paused there for quite some time.

'It is good to see much devotion,' said the Procurator approvingly. 'Say what you like, but the heart of Russia is still in the right place.'

Dmitri was examining the chains. Each length had been filed through neatly in two places. It must have taken some time and could not have been done without at least some noise; and yet Father Kiril, that jealous guardian of the One-Legged Lady's virtue, had been there the whole time and claimed to have remarked nothing.

Here he was hobbling out of the shadows now.

'Eyeing her all over!' he said.

'What?' said the Procurator, startled.

'Just as if she was one of *them*. Disgusting, I call it!'

'I should say so!' said Boris Petrovich warmly. 'And quite inappropriate not to say improper, in a monastery!'

'A curious name for an icon,' commented Volkov when they met later in the afternoon, over the tea and cakes.

'It was named after a curious lady,' said the Father Superior.

'Tell me about her.'

'The One-Legged Lady? Well, as I think I mentioned, she was a pious lady who lived on a small estate near Tula. I say pious, but that was not how she started out.'

'No?'

'No. She was the young wife of an elderly landowner who led a debauched life and very soon, I'm afraid, initiated her into his pleasures. Their names became notorious in the neighbourhood. One night, returning from an orgy —'

The Father Superior paused.

'The peasants like that bit,' he said. 'It makes them feel she was one of them.'

Dmitri smiled. Volkov did not. The Father Superior shrugged his shoulders almost imperceptibly and moved on.

— 'driven by a driver almost as drunk as themselves, they met with an accident.'

He paused again.

'They like that bit, too. It shows that you can't get away with anything; which certainly corresponds to their experience.'

Volkov's face remained expressionless.

'The husband was killed and the wife lay trapped for some hours in the wreckage. She suffered frost-bite and one leg had to be amputated. After that, she was a changed woman – in all senses.'

'Yes,' said Volkov.

'Eyeing her all over –' began Father Kiril.

'Yes, I know,' said Dmitri. 'Disgusting!'

'Show some respect! I said –'

'They do usually, don't they?' said Dmitri.

'Everyone who comes in here –'

'But not him. Why was that, do you think? Because he was not a pilgrim?'

Dmitri had a theory, which was that Father Kiril was more dotty than deaf; or, at any rate, that his deafness was something that could be conveniently turned on or off. Which Father Kiril now confirmed.

'You could tell by the way he looked at her. It was in his eyes. No respect!'

'How many times did he come?'

'Just the once.'

'Was that the night she was taken?'

'No,' said Father Kiril. '"Show some respect" I said.'

'No, of course, it wouldn't have been. It would have been during the day. When it was ordinary for people to be coming and looking at her.'

'"Why don't you bugger off?" he said.'

'You didn't, though, did you?'

'Certainly not!' said Father Kiril. 'He was the one who buggered off.'

'I should think so! He was afraid he was attracting attention, probably. Now, look, you obviously remember him very clearly, why is that? Why did he stand out among all the people coming here?'

'No respect!'

'His manner? Yes, I see that. But was there something else? His clothes, perhaps? How was he dressed? Like a Barin?'

'They're all the same,' said Father Kiril contemptuously.

'But he wasn't the same, surely? Oh, I see. Barins, you mean, they're all the same. But – oh, I've got it: the Barins who came here are all the same?'

'No respect!'

'Interested in the art not religion?'

'These days everyone's a Barin,' said Father Kiril.

'But – oh, I see what you mean. Not a real Barin, you mean?'

Father Kiril nodded vigorously.

'A jumped-up Barin?'

'No respect!'

'No, I know what you mean. Can you remember anything else about him? Face? Hair?'

A look of puzzled concentration came over Father Kiril's face; then went away again.

'Tired,' he said.

'Of course. Another time, perhaps.'

'Bugger off!'

Dmitri wasn't sure whether this was reminiscence or injunction.

'Addled!' said Father Afanesi, tapping his forehead significantly and nodding at Father Kiril's back. 'Cracked!'

'Not altogether,' said Dmitri.

Father Afanesi gave him a quick look.

'No,' he said solemnly, 'perhaps not.'

'Father Afanesi,' said Dmitri, 'have you been here a long time?'

'Long time?' The monk cackled. 'Sixty years,' he said. 'If that counts as a long time! Him and me,' he said, nodding after Father Kiril, 'we've been here longest. But I've been here longer than him!'

'You were here, then, when the One-Legged Lady first came to the Monastery?'

The monk gave him another of his quick looks.

'That's right,' he said. 'I was here before the changes.'

61

'What were the changes? Can you tell me about them?'

'She ought to have stayed up there. That's where she belongs, doesn't she? Tula's not us and we're not Tula. But they won't have it like that.'

'They?' said Dmitri.

'Things changed when she came here. They had to, didn't they? Otherwise there'd be no point.'

First, the *zakuski*, the cold starters: sturgeon of various sorts – the large beluga, the middle-sized sevroga, the small, delicate osyotr; little dishes of cucumber and sour cream; salmon caviar served on pancakes, ordinary caviar piled on eggs in big black and orange heaps.

Then the soup, two sorts, both, Dmitri was pleased to see, light: the dill-flavoured *rassolnik* and the lemon and meaty *solyanka*, accompanied by *pirozhkis*, little pasties filled with chicken and veal and mushrooms.

The main dishes: baby sturgeon in aspic jelly, salmon laid out on ashets, Caspian roach (served with chilled vodka), omul from Lake Baikal: hazel hen served with plums, black-cocks served with saffron, crane sharp with spice; chicken dishes from Georgia, *satsivi* and *chakhokibli*, meat balls from Armenia, turkey from Moldavia.

And after: babas dripping with rum, yoghourts from Azerbaijan, Kazakhstan and Georgia, pyramid-shaped paskha cheeses wrenched out of their normal Easter context.

'If the Church can't be flexible,' said the Father Superior, 'who can?'

The Procurator sat back and eased a button.

'I'm all for flexibility,' he said.

He eased another.

'And yet,' he said, 'you could argue it another way.'

'Oh?'

'Yes. Some would say that the original insistence of the Church that certain foods could not be eaten on certain days held Russian cuisine back, because it restricted the combinations of ingredients that were available to Russian chefs. As compared, say, with those available to chefs in the West.'

'Ah,' said the Father Superior, 'you are a Westernizer?'

'On food,' said the Procurator, with a hasty glance at Volkov. 'Only on food!'

The next morning Volkov continued with his interviews. What he was interviewing the monks about was not altogether clear since they did not talk about it afterwards. But perhaps that was the way of things in a monastery? People seemed to get on with what they were doing and not talk much among themselves. Dmitri had the feeling, however, that the monks were more than usually subdued.

The pilgrims, on the other hand, who seemed to have been having corresponding discussions with the Chief of Police, although in groups and not as individuals, were less subdued than puzzled.

'What did he ask you, Yuri?' Dmitri heard one of them asking.

'Where had I come from; and what was I doing here.'

'Well, that's obvious enough, isn't it?'

'I told him I'd come to see the Old Lady, but he said: "she's not here, is she? So what are you hanging around for?" "In case she comes back," I said. "Well, that's not very likely, is it?" he said. "I don't know," I said. "They say that young Barin's going to find her." So he just snorts and tells me I'm an idle sod.'

'Well, you are, aren't you? But what's that got to do with it?'

'Exactly what I told him. "It's easy to see," I said, "that you've never been hungry." Only I didn't say it to his face, because that would have been asking for trouble, but after he'd gone. But it's true, isn't it?'

'None of them have. They don't really know what it's all about, do they?'

'I don't know why he's asking questions like that. They say that other one is seeing all the monks. I don't know why he's doing that, either.'

'They're running round in circles over the Old Lady going missing.'

'She's certainly stirred them up, hasn't she?'

'Yes, and that's no bad thing. Still, I would have liked to have had a word with her before she left.'

'It's a bit late for that. She'll be half way to Opona by now.'

They were gathering in the Father Superior's room, where there was a samovar similar to the one in the refectory, all blue tiles.

'Lovely, isn't it?' said the Procurator. He bent down and peered at it. 'Eighteenth century?'

'End of,' said the Father Superior. 'My predecessor brought it with him. That one and the one in the refectory. Lemon?'

'Sugar. It's from the Haussenberg factory, isn't it? I've got one myself.'

'You have?' said Volkov.

'Much smaller. And not quite as old, I'm afraid.'

'I've always been fond of it,' said the Father Superior. 'Jam?'

'Please,' said Dmitri.

'And lemon,' said the Father Superior, handing a glass to Volkov.

They took the tea to the table and sat down.

'How have you been getting on?' asked the Father Superior.

Volkov did not reply immediately. He seemed to be still preoccupied with the samovar.

'It came with your predecessor?' he said.

'Yes.'

'Like so many other things,'

'Well, naturally.'

Volkov switched his attention back to the meeting. It was, however, as if he was filing the samovar for future reference.

'Well,' he said to the Chief of Police, 'what have you found?'

'It was as you thought,' said Maximov. 'Over half of them come from Tula.'

'You are referring to the pilgrims, I presume,' said the Father Superior. 'That is hardly surprising. There's famine in the region and they're looking for succour, both spiritual and material.'

'But why come here?' asked Volkov. 'There are plenty of other monasteries which are closer.'

The Father Superior hesitated.

'I think it's perhaps because we're known as one of the wealthier monasteries,' he said, 'and so are thought to be able to be more generous. Also,' he hesitated again, 'perhaps because of our associations.'

'With Tula?'

'With the Kaminski Monastery at Tula.'

'Yes,' said Volkov, 'you have a lot of connections with them, don't you?'

'My predecessor came from there, certainly.'

'And many of the monks.'

'Some of them.'

'You yourself.'

'Initially,' said the Father Superior, 'but then I moved away. I spent fifteen years at the Speransky Monastery at Kiev. And then another three years with the Metropolitan at Moscow before coming here.'

'Youthful years are often the most influential ones,' said Volkov.

'You don't believe in growing up?'

Volkov smiled his wintry smile.

'I believe,' he said, 'that when they were looking for a Superior, you would have seemed a safe choice – a guarantee that the character of the place would be preserved.'

'Continuity of spiritual life is important in a place like this.'

'I wasn't thinking of spiritual life,' said Volkov. 'I was thinking of character.'

'Well, that, too, is important, of course.'

'Especially in a place like this.'

The Father Superior drummed his fingers on the table.

'I fail to see the point you're making.'

Volkov sat back in his chair and looked around him.

'This is a strange place,' he said. 'Sometimes you wonder where it is.'

65

'I beg your pardon?'

'Is it here,' said Volkov, 'or is it at Tula?'

'I hope you are not suggesting that we are merely a copy of Kaminski?'

'Not so much a copy,' said Volkov, 'as a colony.'

'I don't know what you mean,' said the Father Superior. 'The Monastery is an independent foundation and –'

Volkov put up his hand.

'I was speaking of character.'

'Inevitably there will be resemblances and perhaps it is an error to take two successive Superiors from the same place. While our liturgy is universal, there can obviously be differences of emphasis, and it may well be that from time to time change is beneficial, but –'

'I was not thinking of liturgy.'

'What were you thinking of?'

'Character. A monastery's values and attitudes –'

'But surely –'

Volkov held up his hand again.

'– especially where non-theological matters are concerned. How, for instance, it relates to the wider community around it, the way it feeds into that community and draws upon it, the way –' Volkov paused – 'the way it reflects it.'

There was a little silence.

'Are you saying,' demanded the Father Superior, 'that because the Kaminski Monastery happens to be located in an area where there is a history of peasant unrest, it, too, is insurrectionary? Because if you are, let me tell you there is not the slightest foundation for such a belief. Still less,' said the Father Superior hotly, 'is there any foundation for the quite extraordinary supposition that because this monastery has drawn two of its most recent Fathers Superior from the Kaminski, it, too, has a propensity in that direction!'

Volkov merely smiled.

'Even by your own arguments,' said the Father Superior, slightly shakily, 'such a conclusion would not follow. You claimed, if you remember, that a monastery takes at least some of its character from the community that surrounds it.

May I remind you that this area, unlike Tula, does not have a history of peasant unrest.'

'Yet,' said Volkov.

'But this is preposterous!' cried the Father Superior. 'You are surely not suggesting that the Monastery is a nest of insurrectionaries?'

'You do have a lot of people from Tula.'

'But they are here for religious purposes, spiritual purposes – they are monks and pilgrims!'

'And you do have the One-Legged Lady.'

'But –'

'Or had.'

'But it's just an icon!'

'A very special one, I think you said. Named after a very special lady. You were telling me about her, if you remember. You said that after her accident she was a changed woman. In what way was she changed?'

'From then on she devoted her life to good works.'

'What sort of works?'

'She made bequests to monasteries.'

'Well, that's all right.'

'She went on pilgrimage, walking from monastery to monastery –'

'On one leg?'

'Yes. It was what she deserved, she said. Two would have been too easy.'

'A sort of penance?'

'Yes.'

'All right, so far,' said Volkov.

'Good. Anyway, one day as she was walking along she came upon some people lying by the roadside. There was famine in the land and they were starving. She sent back to her house for food and – well, I think the rest you know.'

'Did she say anything?'

'Say anything?'

'Like, well, that it wasn't their fault?'

'I don't know. The records are silent on that point.'

'A pity,' said Volkov thoughtfully. 'It would have been

useful to know.' He considered for a while. 'Good works are all right,' he said at last.

'Oh, good.'

'In principle, I mean.'

'Well, yes.'

'So long as they are not carried to excess.'

'She fed a lot of people,' said the Father Superior. 'Does that count as excess?'

'It could. It depends what she said as she travelled through the seditious areas.'

'You are surely not suggesting that the One-Legged Lady was an insurrectionary?'

'I think it is worth investigating,' said Volkov, 'in view of the tradition that has come down.'

'But – but this is just history!' cried the Father Superior.

'Everything has to have a beginning and it may be that the roots of the present situation lie here. In the Corps of Gendarmes,' said Volkov, 'we learn to look behind things.'

'But –'

'Besides, aren't you forgetting something? The Lady herself may be history but her embodiment lives on.'

'The – the Icon?'

'With all its seditious potential.'

'You are surely not suggesting –?'

'I am not suggesting anything,' said Volkov. 'Not just at the moment. I am wondering, that is all: wondering why, of all monasteries, you should choose to reflect the character of the one at Tula; why of all icons, you should choose to acquire and promote an icon with the associations that the One-Legged Lady has; and why, at the very moment when those associations are coming alive again, that particular icon – that particular icon! – should disappear.'

6

Dmitri's difficult grandfather did not hold with icons. Consistent to his eighteenth-century rationalism, he regarded them as superstitious relics and would not have them in the house. Vera Samsonova would have been proud of him.

It had been a bone of contention with Dmitri's mother, an orthodox member of the Russian Orthodox Church, who, mild in everything else, had been firm on this, that whatever her father-in-law might think, there were definitely going to be icons in *her* house. Called on to mediate between them, Dmitri's father had ruled that how one furnished one's house was a matter of taste only; which satisfied neither of them. His own position remained unknown. Since there were no icons in the Scottish Presbyterian Church, he pointed out, the question did not arise.

Dmitri had not grown up, then, in a household in which icons had played an unquestioned part and he found it hard to conceive a life in which they did. The monks, yes, with a stretch of the imagination he could guess how they might feel about holy images. But the peasants? With their strange combination of earthy realism and apparent devotion? How did icons, he asked himself, as he stood listening to the deep-voiced singing and looking at the icons spread out on the iconostasis in front of him, fit into their lives? Was it possible for them to serve, as Volkov seemed to suppose, as a focus for feelings other than religious?

'You make it sound as if we are part of some conspiracy!' the Father Superior had protested that afternoon.

Volkov had merely shrugged.

'Your word,' he had said. But, really, that was what he had been implying.

'You have no basis for such a suggestion!' The Father Superior had said hotly. 'Where is your evidence?'

And then, as Volkov had hesitated, the Father Superior had pressed home his advantage. 'Where is your evidence?'

'The Icon —'

'Has been used for religious purposes only. Show me your evidence that it has been used for anything else!'

Volkov had hesitated again.

'You cannot. And that is because there is no such evidence. It is all,' the Father Superior had said contemptuously, 'the product of your own sick fantasy.'

Volkov had not liked that.

'We shall see,' he had said, and had got up from the table.

The Father Superior had won a victory of sorts; but he had been left under no illusion.

'What shall I do?' he had whispered, after Volkov had gone. 'Once they have got their teeth into you, they don't let go.'

'You've got to make him see that it's not the way he thinks.' Dmitri had said.

The Father Superior had shaken his head.

'Once they think in a particular way,' he said, 'they don't change their minds.'

'You've got to make them see that it's just a simple theft.'

'It was that once,' said the Father Superior despondently. 'It's not that now.'

'If it was that once,' said Dmitri doggedly, 'then it's that now.'

'Not if that's not the way that they see it,' the Father Superior had said. 'It's the way that they see it that counts.'

Dmitri knew that there was an awful truth in what the Father Superior had said. Once the Russian state, with its vast bureaucracy, had adopted an official view on something, it did not, perhaps could not, change its mind.

But it was a truth that he resisted. It was not the way that officials defined things that made them real. They were as they were. If this was a simple theft, then it was a simple theft. If, of course, it was a simple theft.

*   *   *

'What shall I do?' the Father Superior had whispered again.

'You've got to show them that it's just a simple theft,' Dmitri had persisted.

'I'd hoped you were going to do that.'

'I still am.' Dmitri had said.

He still was; only, he thought, as he gazed at the icons blinking on the iconostasis in front of him, it wasn't quite so simple.

The space that the One-Legged Lady had occupied was still raw. The chains which once had bound her had been left hanging down on either side. There was something about them that troubled Dmitri.

They had been cut the night she was taken. Well, that was possible. The bights were thick, certainly, and it would have taken some time, but it could have been done. And then the heavy icon had been lifted down and carried away. Well, that was possible, too, although it probably would have required several men.

And all this had been done without Father Kiril hearing or seeing a thing! Dmitri suddenly realised what was troubling him. That was impossible. The old man was jealous in his guardianship of the One-Legged Lady; and, confused and eccentric though he may be, on anything touching her he could have missed nothing.

Incense began to drift out from behind the iconostasis and the deep-voiced singing started again. The service was coming to an end. Behind him the pilgrims stood rapt. Boris Petrovich, his nose tickled by the incense, stifled a sneeze. Beyond him Maximov stared stolidly into space: and beyond him, his white gloves tucked neatly into the belt of his immaculate blue tunic, stood Volkov, meticulous in the observance of this, as of all other of the Tsar's decreed formalities.

'Disgusting, I call it!' said Dmitri.

Father Kiril was thrown off balance.

'Disgusting?'

'Taking the chains off her.'

71

'Keep them in chains, I say!' thundered Father Kiril.

'Otherwise, they'll be off down to the fields.'

'At it!' said Father Kiril with relish. 'I've seen them!'

'The Old Lady?'

The monk looked at him in astonishment.

'The peasant girls.'

'Oh, but they weren't in chains.'

'What are you on about?' said the old man.

Dmitri tried again.

'The Old Lady,' he said. 'They shouldn't have done it. Taken the chains off, I mean.'

'Down to the fields,' growled Father Kiril. 'They're all the same.'

'Quite so. It was a mistake to take the chains off. I'll bet you said something to them.'

'Said something?'

'Yes. That night. What were they doing there anyway, in the dark? That's not right!'

'Dark?' said the old man. He seemed puzzled.

'Yes. That night. When they cut the chains.'

Father Kiril seemed to be struggling.

'Not night,' he brought out at last.

'Not night? But –?'

'Day,' said Father Kiril

Dmitri's hopes took a fall.

'I know it's day now. But it wasn't then. Not when they took the chains off.'

'Day,' said Father Kiril obstinately.

'The night they took the chains off.'

'Not night,' said Father Kiril firmly. 'Day.'

Dmitri sighed inwardly. How was he going to get round this? Perhaps the best thing was to leave it and try again another time.

'Work during the night?' said Father Kiril. 'Him? You'll be lucky!'

'Him?' said Dmitri. 'Them. There must have been more than one of them.'

Father Kiril shook his head.

'He's the one with the tools.'

'Tools?'

'You need tools for a job like this.'

'Are you saying – are we talking about the same thing? Cutting the chains?'

Father Kiril nodded his head vigorously.

'"It's a mistake," I said. "You don't want to do that. She'll be off. She's no better than the rest of them."'

'The One-Legged Lady? Are we talking about the One-Legged Lady?'

'"She'll be off," I said. "Down to the fields. With the others."'

'It wasn't done that night? Not the night she was taken? But –'

'They're all the same,' said Father Kiril, slipping back into confusion.

'Beautiful, aren't they?' said Boris Petrovich.

Dmitri spun round. The Procurator was standing right behind him. He nodded towards the icons.

He went up to the iconostasis and stopped in front of an icon that Dmitri had not noticed before.

'This is my favourite,' he said.

It showed the face of a young girl, the Virgin somebody-or-other, and had an unusual delicacy of colour. The metal plate which covered half the face was cut back at the top to reveal some extraordinarily secular curls and Dmitri thought he could see exactly why the icon appealed to the Procurator.

'I have an aesthetic eye, you know,' said Boris Petrovich. 'My wife says so, at least. "You have the eye of an artist, Boris Petrovich," she says.'

'That's why I chose you, my dear,' I say. Returning the compliment, you know. But, really, she is quite striking. So is Ariadne.'

'Ariadne?'

'Our daughter. You haven't met her? Dear, dear, that must be put right. You will be impressed. She's growing into a real beauty.'

'Isn't she still at school?'

'That was last year. Still at school?' Boris Petrovich chuckled,

'Oh, dear, no, Dmitri Alexandrovich. She's very much the woman now. As you will find. So poised, so accomplished.' The Procurator sighed. 'That, of course, is part of the trouble.'

'Trouble?'

'Accomplishment has to be paid for. Tutors for this, tutors for that. Bills every day. So the Father Superior was quite right.'

'I beg your pardon?'

'About the icon. I wouldn't be able to afford it.'

'This icon here?'

Dmitri looked at the Virgin again.

'Yes.'

'You asked if you could buy it?'

'Well, not quite like that. "If you ever think of getting rid of it," I said to the Father Superior, "let me know." "I'm afraid you're well down in the queue, Boris Petrovich," he said. "There are others ahead of you. His Excellency, the Governor, for one. But in any case it would be out of your reach. Out of his, too, for that matter. We could get a high price for something like this. We'd take it straight to Marputin."'

To Dmitri's irritation, the Procurator fell into step beside him as they left the Chapel.

'Dmitri Alexandrovich,' he said in a confidential whisper, 'there was something I wanted to ask you.'

'Yes?'

'What shall I do?'

'Do?'

'Yes. About the samovar.'

'Samovar?'

'The one I have at home. It's exactly like the one the Father Superior has in his room. It comes from Tula, too. I wish I hadn't said that when Volkov was listening, Tula's a bad place to have anything to do with just at the moment.'

'I wouldn't have thought –'

'Ought I to get rid of it, do you think? I wouldn't want to get dragged into – well, all this. I'm not thinking of myself, of course. My wife, Ariadne and . . . and the office. Yes, the office. It would look bad for a senior official – the Law should be above these things, you know, I've always felt that. So what shall I do, Dmitri Alexandrovich? About the samovar? Give it away?'

'Give it away, by all means,' said Dmitri indifferently. Inspiration suddenly came to him. 'Give it to Sonya Milusovich.'

'Sonya Milusovich?'

'To help with the famine.'

'Do you think they'd want a samovar?' said Boris Petrovich doubtfully.

'Tell her to sell it and use the money for famine relief. That would look good, Boris Petrovich. It would help you with your election campaign for the Zemstvo.'

As soon as he could, he shook him off and went back to the Chapel. At first, when he looked at the ends of the cut links, he could not see anything; they had been wiped so clean. Disappointed, he dropped on his knees and there, among the candle-grease and sawdust, along with the dust that had fallen when the iron links had been filed through, he found what he was looking for: droppings of wax.

He looked at the links again and this time, on two of the cut surfaces where the wiping had been imperfect, he found the faint traces.

Although the snow in the Monastery-yard was trodden hard and grey, beyond the gates it was clean and soft. There had been a fresh fall in the night which had restored the surrounding fields to their pristine whiteness and covered the track to the depth of a few inches. The pilgrims' boots sank into it as they trudged towards the Monastery.

Almost everyone who visited the Monastery came on foot. Only the well-to-do had sleighs and they tended to reserve their pilgrimages for the warmer months. In the past four or five weeks, said Father Sergei at the gates, very few people had come to the Monastery by sleigh. He could almost enumerate them: the Father Superior of a neighbouring monastery, the Bishop, the Governor, Dmitri, Volkov. He could not recall anyone answering to the description Dmitri gave him.

75

Dmitri was fairly sure, however, that the nattily-dressed man whom Avdotya Feodorovna had described, the not-quite Barin of both hers and Father Kiril's account, would not have come in any other way. He did not see him trudging through the snow.

Had he got it wrong? Perhaps they were not the same man after all. Or perhaps Father Kiril's encounter with his respect-lacking visitor had taken place longer ago than he supposed.

Outside in the yard there was suddenly an altercation. Voices were raised. Some of them sounded oddly familiar.

Father Sergei sprang to his feet.

'It's Grusha again! Really –'

It was, indeed, Grusha again. This time she appeared to have collided with Nikita, the carter, coming in at the gate with a load of logs. The two wagons were jammed together in the gateway.

'You stupid bastard!' she was shouting. 'Couldn't you get out of the way?'

'With a load like this? What do you think this is? A droshky?'

'You could see me coming!'

'No, I bloody couldn't! What were you doing, swinging round like that?'

'I had to swing round, didn't I? This daft bastard has parked his sleigh right in the way.'

'Why didn't you look? You would have seen me coming.'

'I was swinging round, wasn't I? How could I bloody look when I was swinging round?'

'You should have looked first!'

'Oh, yes? And how do you think I could have done that from up here? Do you think I've got a bloody rubber neck or something?'

'You've got a bloody wooden head!'

'I've got a bloody wooden boot,' shouted Grusha, beginning to climb down, 'which I'm going to put up your ass!'

'Oh, are you?' shouted the carter, getting ready to jump down. 'We'll see about that, you drunken old bitch!'

'Grusha! Nikita!' cried Father Sergei, running towards them.

From all over the yard people came running.

'I'll bloody kill you!' shouted Grusha, and leaped to the ground. Whereupon her feet slid from under her and she crashed heavily down on her back.

'I'll show you what a boot's for!' shouted the carter, swinging himself down but then finding himself unable to get at her because the carts were in the way. Jammed together, they formed a solid wall.

'You stupid bitch!' cried the carter, running from one end to the other, trying to find a way through.

'Brother, brother!' remonstrated one of the pilgrims, trying to catch him by the arm. Nikita shook him off. He grabbed Grusha's horse by the head and tried to tug it through to make a gap. The horse whinnied and reared and became more securely wedged. The carter beat on the cart with his fists in impotent fury.

'Brother, brother!'

Several pilgrims rushed up and seized him.

'Remember she is your sister!'

'She's a bloody cabbage!' shouted the carter.

His own horses, on the other side of the gates, panicked, too, and began to thrash around. The cart lurched and some logs fell off.

'Jesus!' cried the carter, as one of them hit him on the foot.

'Mother of God!' echoed Grusha faintly on the other side of the carts, as logs began to rain round her.

Father Sergei pulled her away.

'Grusha!' he said. 'Grusha! Are you all right!'

'I'm bloody dead,' she said. 'That bastard has killed me!' she opened her eyes. 'And now I'm going to bloody kill him!'

She tried to get to her feet but reeled and fell back.

'I feel sick,' she said.

'I'm not surprised,' said someone.

It was her friend from the kitchen.

'Have you been giving her drink again?' said Father Sergei, furious.

'Just a drop. At least, it would have been a drop if she hadn't got hold of the bottle.'

'Grusha, this won't do!' said Father Sergei sternly. 'It's beginning to happen too often. If it happens again we'll have to make some other arrangement.'

'It wasn't my fault!' whined Grusha. 'It was his! He was driving without due care. It's my belief he's had more than he should have!'

'I haven't even got here yet!' shouted the carter, from the other side of the wagons.

'Keep him out, Father!' advised Grusha. 'He's a sinful man. He beats his wife something cruel.'

'I'll bloody beat you!' shouted the carter.

'And his horses. You wouldn't believe, Father, how he treats those horses!'

The carter broke free, seized a log and threw it at her.

'Mary, Mother of God!' cried Grusha. 'You see the man he is!'

The pilgrims seized the carter again and dragged him off to one side.

'Can we get those carts out of the way?' called the Father Superior. He had come into the yard, along, it seemed, with most of the monks, and, indeed, most of the Monastery. The Procurator was there, the Chief of Police, shouldering his way through the pilgrims, even Volkov, aloof at the back of the crowd.

Maximov arrived at the gates.

'Anyone know about horses?' he demanded.

'Nikita does,' said the carpenter, who had come out to see the fun.

'Nikita does, does he? Well, where the hell is he? Nikita!?'

'Here!' said the carter sheepishly from the other side of the carts. He had quietened down now.

'What do we do about these horses?'

'Unhitch them. Hers first.'

'Right. Now come on, some of you –'

Several of the pilgrims stepped forward. The carter pushed them aside and went up to Grusha's cart himself.

'He's a good man, really,' whispered Grusha confidingly.

'A bit too fond of the drink, that's all it is.' She put her hand to her head. 'As a matter of fact, I could just do with a drop myself.' She looked at Father Sergei. 'You don't think, Father –?'

'No,' said Father Sergei.

'Oh, well,' she said, flopping back. 'He's a dear, good man, as I say. It wasn't his fault. Nor mine either. It was that daft bastard who parked his sleigh in the wrong place.'

'Grusha!' said someone warningly.

'They're always doing that. No more sense than a rabbit.'

'Grusha –'

'It was the same with the Governor the other day. 'You daft bastard!' I said. 'Don't you know how to park a sleigh? Or, at least, when to come out and when not to.' I mean, this yard's like a sheet of ice, and if you've got a heavy load up, you can't just stop or turn, not just like that. It was for him to stop, not me. I mean, all he had to do was wait. It was his fault. "You daft old bastard," I said. "Now look at my cabbages!" They were all over the yard. Did he stop and help? No, he did not. Just drove away, his nose stuck in the air, like the great ponce he is –'

'Grusha –'

'They're all like that,' she said, enjoying herself. 'Just because they own everything else, they think they own the road. Drive like madmen, park anywhere. No thought for other people. Just look at that daft bastard who's parked his sleigh over there –'

She looked up and saw the Chief of Police, and the white gloves and the blue tunic of Volkov just behind him.

'Oh, my God!' she said, falling back. 'They're coming for me already!'

'She was right about one thing, though,' the man from the kitchen was saying, as the yard began to clear. 'It wasn't her fault. Not that time! He was too impatient, you see. He wouldn't wait. Went right into her. The driver went flying, His Excellency went ass over tit, there was a bloke in the sleigh with them, he went flying too. Finished up in the snow with the cabbages all round him. A bit of a dresser, he was, so that didn't suit him. And then there was Grusha, standing up there on her cart, giving them lip. It was a right to-do. I can tell you. But worth seeing. The Father Superior had to take His Excellency in and give him a drink. You know, to put things right. Him and the other chap who was with him. I took the driver into the kitchen. "It serves you right," I said. "You weren't thinking what you were doing. It's a sheet of ice out there. You can't expect her to twist and turn, not with a cart –"'

'Someone will have to speak to her,' said the Father Superior. 'We can't have this going on. It happens all the time. Only the other day, His Excellency –'

'Yes,' said Dmitri. 'His Excellency.'

'Well, it was most unpleasant. He was very angry. He wanted to know what I was doing employing a woman like that. "I don't really employ her." I said. "She's more of a force of nature." I had to open one of my best bottles.'

'He had someone with him, I believe?'

'That made it worse. His first visit to the Monastery, and there he was tumbled about with the cabbages!'

'A friend of the Governor's?'

'I imagine so. I didn't really speak to him much. When we were talking about the fund – the dome needs touching up, you know – he remained outside. Said he would like to visit the Chapel. And then, afterwards, of course, I was so hot and bothered – I mean, suppose he had broken his back? – that all I could do was try and calm His Excellency down and get as much liquor into them as I could.'

'You didn't gather his name?'

'Korol, was it? Something like that. Yes, Korol, I think.'

'And His Excellency didn't explain who he was?'

'Just come along for the ride, I think. He said he was interested in monasteries and had heard so much about ours.'

'Did he mention icons?'

'Icons? No, I don't think so. Why?'

'I thought he might be interested in icons.'

'Well, that would explain it. Explain why he was with the Governor, I mean. His Excellency is very interested in icons.'

*   *   *

Dmitri went back out into the yard. Volkov's driver was standing by his sleigh getting ready to depart. Volkov had announced that they would be leaving in ten minutes. He was having a last word with the Father Superior.

Dmitri wandered down to the gates. A group of pilgrims, their staves in their hands and their bundles on their backs, was just saying farewell to Father Sergei.

Their bundles seemed bulkier than usual.

'Now, lads,' Father Sergei was saying, 'remember: some for your family, some for your neighbour. It's not a lot but it's the best we can do.'

They knelt to receive his blessing.

'Far to go?' asked Dmitri.

'Not far. Tula.'

'Not as far as Opona,' said someone.

They all laughed.

Volkov emerged with the Father Superior, who looked pale but self-possessed.

'I'll see you again shortly,' said Volkov.

'Yes, I'm sure,' said the Father Superior, depressed.

They all climbed into the sleigh. Volkov sat at one end, Boris Petrovich, Maximov and Dmitri, a trifle uncomfortably, at the other. The driver cracked his whip and the big sleigh began to glide, slowly at first until it got through the gates, but then with increasing speed over the snow.

'You've got good horses, Your Excellency,' said Maximov appreciatively.

Volkov nodded.

'I daresay you need them. You do a lot of travelling, I expect?'

Volkov nodded again.

'Russia's a big country,' said Maximov sagely.

It was, indeed, thought Dmitri, a big country. It would take the pilgrims several days to reach Tula, let alone – what was that other place they kept mentioning? – Opona.

'How far is Opona?' asked Dmitri.

Volkov jumped as if he had been shot.

7

'Where did you hear that word?' said Volkov sharply.

'In general conversation.'

'Among whom?'

'The peasants,' said Dmitri reluctantly.

'At the Monastery?'

'Yes.'

Volkov sighed.

'Where *is* Opona?' asked Dmitri.

'Nowhere. It doesn't exist. But the peasants think it does. They think it's a kingdom somewhere at the edge of the flat earth where peasants can live in happiness without any interference by state or gentry. It's a myth,' said Volkov, 'which resurfaces every time there is trouble in the country-side.'

'It was usually just a casual remark,' said Dmitri. 'Like, "It's a long way to Opona".'

'Well, yes,' said Volkov. 'But it came up several times?'

'Yes.'

'In what context?'

'Usually, as I said, distance. Icons, sometimes,' said Dmitri remembering.

'Icons? Any icon in particular?'

'The One-Legged Lady,' said Dmitri reluctantly.

Volkov was silent for some time. Then he said: 'I was afraid so.'

'I don't think it meant anything particular,' said Dmitri. 'It was just: "She'll be half-way to Opona by now."'

'You don't think that means anything?'

'Well –'

'It means,' said Volkov, 'that she's in their hands, for them to do with as they wish.'

He lapsed into gloomy silence.

Maximov cleared his throat.

'Excellency –'

'Yes?'

'Excellency, I wondered if Dmitri Alexandrovich was able to identify any of them? If he was, I'd soon beat the truth out of them.'

'No,' said Dmitri.

'No,' said Volkov, after reflecting. 'Our peasants are like oxes; the more you beat them, the more obstinate they get. We'll have to be more subtle.'

He sat there thinking.

'Would you say that the road to Opona led through Tula?' he asked Dmitri suddenly.

'I think it might.'

'I think it might, too. We're going to have to send someone there.' He looked at Dmitri. 'You.'

'My concern is purely with the theft of the One-Legged Lady –' objected Dmitri quickly.

'And that is what you will be investigating. It will be good cover.'

'This is where the Icon was stolen,' said Dmitri.

'But you're trying to recover it, aren't you?'

'I doubt if I'll find it at Tula.'

'I doubt if you'll find it there too,' conceded Volkov, 'yet.'

Dmitri thought of other objections. Volkov waved them aside.

'Consider yourself attached to the Corps of the Gendarmes,' he said.

The last thing Dmitri wanted was to be attached to the Corps of Gendarmes. For one thing it was the way to lose all your friends. For another, he had seen enough of the Tsar's special police forces when he was in Siberia to know that they were not for him.

Besides, he was convinced that it would be a waste of time. The theft had taken place here and not in Tula. And all this talk of a peasant uprising was beside the point. In Dmitri's view it was about as likely as the land of Opona itself. What the problem was, was plain: it was the famine. And that wasn't a thing for security police or law officers, it was a thing for, well, yes, Vera Samsonova was probably right, the local Zemstvo. Not for Uncle Vlady, perhaps, who couldn't even solve a crossword puzzle. But for someone more competent. Certainly not for the Corps of Gendarmes. And even more certainly, not for him.

He was, as he had told Volkov, concerned narrowly with the law. That was difficult enough. One of the things that made it difficult was that in Russia questions of law had a way of broadening out and becoming questions of order which in turn quickly became questions of politics and of whose side you were on, the Tsar's or everyone else's.

It wasn't so much that Dmitri was on the side of everyone else as that he was on the side, passionately on the side, of the law itself. That was something new in Russia. Twenty years before, a reforming Tsar had created for the first time in Russia a legal system that was independent; or, more accurately, a system with the possibility of being independent. It had independent judges (fairly), independent juries (up to a point and sometimes awkwardly beyond it: 'let's have justice, and never mind about the law.') and a new breed of professional, independent lawyers, of whom Dmitri was one.

Unfortunately, the reforming Tsar had been assassinated and his successor, not surprisingly, had reacted strongly. He had clamped down heavily on all the reforms that had just been introduced and built up the police state to unprecedented levels. In the new climate, the embryonic legal system had to fight for its life and it was touch and go whether it would succeed. Dmitri was one of those who believed it had to succeed. This, in his view, was Russia's last chance of achieving a democratic society. Not Vera Samsonova's zemstvos.

The Corps of Gendarmes represented for him everything that was wrong with the Tsarist system. Association with it would be association with everything he was fighting against.

Temporary though it would be, he felt that it would leave him tainted.

But how was he going to get out of it? Simply refuse? You didn't refuse the Corps of Gendarmes, not if you didn't want to go to Siberia.

The only way was somehow to show Volkov that he was barking up the wrong tree, that the disappearance of the One-Legged Lady was a question only of simple theft, that all this stuff about an uprising was, as the Father Superior had said, pure fantasy.

But how was he going to do that if he was at Tula? There were things here that he needed to find out about. He was just beginning to get somewhere and now – now he would have to drop it all!

His friends received the news as badly as he had feared.

'So, Dmitri,' said Vera Samsonova nastily, 'you've found your right berth at last!'

'If you'd listened to us,' said Igor Stepanovich, 'this would never have happened.'

'At least,' said Sonya, 'you can take some of our parcels with you.'

The parcels included Uncle Vlady.

'Hasn't he got his own sleigh?' asked Dmitri.

'No,' said Sonya, 'he'd have to borrow ours. And since you're going anyway –'

'Even with the parcels,' said Igor Stepanovich, 'there's plenty of room.'

Much less room than had originally appeared. More and more bags were brought out of Sonya's parents' living room until the sleigh was piled high with them.

The sleigh had in any case been a vexed issue.

'Of course you must go by sleigh!' said Volkov angrily. 'This is urgent!'

He had naturally not offered his own.

'Take the Court one,' he had said loftily.

Boris Petrovich had protested.

'But I need it,' he said, 'for my duties.'

For his social life, thought Dmitri privately. However,

85

hoping that this would prove an insurmountable stumbling block, he had looked grave and muttered 'ah, yes, the duties!'

'Hire one, then,' said Volkov, vaulting with ease the insurmountable.

'But – but – who will pay?' Boris Petrovich had stammered.

'You will,' said Volkov.

Dmitri had pointed out to the Procurator that it would cost the office much less if he let Dmitri have the court-house sleigh and hired one himself from the cab rank outside the Metropole whenever he needed one. Boris Petrovich had yielded with ill grace and so Dmitri had finally taken possession of the sleigh and driver, who was necessary but not an asset.

'You're not expecting me to take this lot!' he had said, reeling back.

But then, as Igor Stepanovich had pointed out, he was reeling anyway.

'I'm sure you won't mind,' said Sonya, 'when you know that it's for the starving of Tula.'

The driver did mind. Famine, he said, was not court-house business; and he could be used only for proper court-house business. Dmitri had then reminded him that on this occasion he was not on court-house business but on business of the Corps of Gendarmes; and that if he had any further objections, perhaps he could put them to that body. The driver was silenced but not mollified, until Vera Samsonova very sensibly brought him out some more of what he had had too much of already.

'Just be careful of the parcels,' she said, pointedly excluding Dmitri from the area of her concern.

The driver grinned.

'Don't worry, Miss,' he said. 'I drive better when I'm drunk.'

'From what I have seen of your ordinary driving,' said Dmitri, 'that must be true.'

It was on the whole a mercy when they finally got going.

Not a fruit bowl, this time, but a condiment set. Two twisted pepper pots spiralling upwards with a salt cellar in between.

Further back, two bulgy-bottomed, tapering-topped flasks, one for the salad dressing, one for the vinegar. The roof was not as brightly coloured, though, nor as freshly painted as at the other monastery. The Kaminski was obviously less well endowed by rich patrons.

Again, though, there was the dark smudge of pilgrims. Or perhaps this time they really were beggars. There were scores of them. For the most part they were sitting listlessly in the yard. A small but steady stream, however, was entering the main Monastery building.

'Where are they going?' asked Dmitri.

'To pray to the One-Legged Lady,' said the friendly monk who had welcomed them.

'The One-Legged Lady?' said Dmitri.

'Yes. Perhaps you've never heard of her. She was a lady who lived not far from here in the last century –'

'I've heard of her,' said Dmitri. 'But –?'

The monk led him into the chapel. Just in front of the iconostasis a flagstone had been raised and some wooden steps led down into the crypt below.

'Would you like –?' the monk invited with his hand.

Dmitri went down the steps. The crypt was full of pilgrims. A cold musty smell hung over everything.

Everywhere there were little boxes, sometimes piled high to the ceiling. One or two had cracked open and inside Dmitri caught a glimpse of something that looked like brown or yellow wood, shrivelled, shrunken.

Most of the pilgrims were clustered in one corner before a box whose lid had been raised. The friendly monk beckoned him forward.

Inside was a little old lady; or, rather, not so much an old lady as a carved statue of one. The tiny brown hands were marvelously done, the stick-like arms delicately folded. The face was like a walnut, brown, small, tight and shrunk into itself. Even the fabric in which she was dressed seemed real, although so faded and fragile that it seemed as if a breath would blow it off. Most realistic of all, at the lower end of the fabric, not two feet peeped out but one.

'The One-Legged Lady,' said the monk proudly.

'Of Kursk?'

The monk looked pained.

'We say: "of Kaminski". Kursk is where the Icon is. We have the body.'

'The – the genuine body?'

'Certainly. You can see. Look!'

He pointed to where the missing leg would have been.

'What happened to the leg?'

'No one knows. Some say,' the monk fluttered his hands deprecatingly, 'that when it was parted from the lady, it set off of its own accord and walked to the Kingdom of Opona.'

'Opona?'

'Some say.'

Dmitri looked round him. The pilgrims were gazing at the little, carved-statue-like figure, intently. Some were muttering a prayer.

'Of course,' said the monk uneasily, 'they are not really praying to her. That would be theologically unsound.'

'Never mind about it being theologically unsound,' said Dmitri. 'It's political unsoundness that you've got to worry about.'

'Of course, we've heard about the theft of the Icon,' said the Father Superior of the Kaminski, 'and we greatly deplore it. But somehow –' he shrugged – 'well, it was a long time ago that it was here and we've lost any feeling that it belongs to us. We don't feel very involved. Except –' he smiled – 'that I have to admit to a certain malicious satisfaction – which, naturally, as a Christian I'm doing my best to fight against – that their ill luck is our good fortune.'

'How so?'

'Well, far more people are coming to see the body now. In the Russian Church relics do not have quite the role that they do in some other churches. It's the icon – the Holy Image – that people want to see. So we've rather lost out by comparison with our friends. There's no doubt that it was a very good move on their part, financially, I mean, and we've suffered by comparison. But now that the Icon has disappeared, people are coming to us in droves. If it goes on like this we might even be able to get the roof painted.'

In the yard Dmitri saw a familiar face. It was Ivan, the big peasant he had encountered on his first visit to the Monastery at Kursk – the one who had complained to the Father Superior about his dissatisfaction over the One-Legged Lady's disappearance. He greeted Dmitri like an old friend.

'Why, Barin, what brings you here?' Then his face clouded over. 'They've not flogged off the body too?'

'No, no,' said Dmitri hastily. 'No.'

'Well, I'm glad to hear that. You never know these days. But I suppose in time of famine everyone gets pinched. Including monasteries.'

'It's all right,' Dmitri assured him. 'As far as I know, they've no intention of getting rid of her. Rather the reverse, in fact.'

'Price gone up, has it?' said the peasant shrewdly. 'Now that the other one has gone.'

'A bit like that, yes.'

'Wouldn't be surprised if they were up here soon making an offer.'

'It wouldn't be the same, though, would it?'

'Well, no. And, besides, it wouldn't be right. This is where she belongs. Both of them. In Tula. And this is where she's needed.'

Dmitri asked him how things were going.

'They're getting worse,' said the big peasant forthrightly. 'If there was little before, there's nothing now. In my village it's acorn soup for all now.'

'I've brought some things down,' said Dmitri. 'You'll be able to sell them.'

'The trouble with that,' said Ivan, 'is that the moneylender gets half the price. Still, I'm not saying it won't be welcome. Anything's better than nothing.'

Dmitri asked him about the position generally. Other villages, said Ivan, were in even an worse plight.

'Over at Zapolonye they're down to eating the straps

round their boots. We've not got to that yet at Yabloki Sad.'

Yabloki Sad? Apple Garden? The name rang a bell. But in what connection Dmitri could not think.

Nor could he think what he was supposed to be doing here. Looking for evidence of peasant unrest? From what he could see, the famine had already taken things beyond that. The peasants in the yard, sitting slumped, unheeding, in the snow, looked too weak to be capable of causing any trouble even if they had wanted to. Besides they seemed to be thinking entirely in other terms. A line of people was standing patiently outside the chapel waiting for their turn to go in.

'I'd best get over there to join them,' said Ivan, 'now that I'm here. It's not the same thing, of course, but it'll have to do. One way or another, we've got to get the Old Lady working for us.'

Over by the wall the driver was unloading the sleigh. Half of the packages were already standing in the snow. Uncle Vlady hovered among them wringing his hands. When he saw Dmitri, he rushed up to him.

'What am I going to do?' he cried. 'How am I going to get all these to Tula?'

'Can't you get the Zemstvo to send a cart?'

'But –'

Impatiently, Dmitri strode into the Monastery gate-house.

'Have you got anything going in to Tula? A cart, perhaps? Or could I send a message to the Zemstvo?'

'The Zemstvo?' said the monk doubtfully. 'Well, I don't know that it would be much good –'

The driver came into the gate-house carrying a bag.

'From Father Sergei,' he said.

'Father Sergei? Oh, right.'

The monk put the bag on the floor.

'You know Father Sergei?' said Dmitri.

'Oh, yes. Everyone knows Father Sergei. He comes from these parts. His father used to be priest over at – where was it? Zapolonye, I think – yes, Zapolonye. He still has family over there. He often sends things up for them.'

'What am I going to do?' wailed Uncle Vlady.

'Is there a cart going in?' asked Dmitri. If the rest of the Zemstvo were like Uncle Vlady he had no great hopes for the success of Sonya's mission.

'Not today,' said the monk.

'What can I do?' cried Uncle Vlady.

'You'll have to take our sleigh,' said Dmitri.

'What?' said the driver.

'It's not far, is it?'

'Less than an hour,' said the monk.

'But, Dmitri Alexandrovich!' cried the driver.

'What's the matter?'

'I'd have to load up the sleigh again!'

'Well?'

'Kaminski was what was said: Nothing was said about Tula!'

'It's the same thing.'

'Begging your pardon, Dmitri Alexandrovich, but it's not at all the same thing. We're working for the Corps of Gendarmes now. I can't go running around on private errands.'

'It's not a private errand. It's for the Zemstvo.'

'The Zemstvo!' the driver laughed derisively. 'Pardon me, Dmitri Alexandrovich, but, with respect, the Zemstvo is one thing and the Corps of Gendarmes quite another. Suppose I was called on for duty by the Corps and I wasn't here? Where would I be? I'd be in bloody Siberia, that's where I'd be!'

'You're not going to be called upon for duty. I'm the only one who's calling on you for duty. And the duty is to take him into Tula.'

'But, Dmitri Alexandrovich,' cried the driver desperately, searching around, 'have you thought about the horses?'

'What about the horses?'

'They're dying for a feed.'

'Well, give them one, then.'

'But, Dmitri Alexandrovich, it will take time!'

'About half an hour,' said the monk.

'Just long enough for you to pick up the packages,' said Dmitri. 'Get on with it!'

At the last moment, Dmitri went up to the sleigh and took some of the packages out.

'I'll need these,' he said. 'And you, too, when you get back.'

When Ivan came out of the chapel Dmitri was waiting for him.

'How did it go?'

Ivan stroked his beard.

'I don't know,' he said. 'I was watching her all the time I was telling her about it to see if she was listening, but she kept her eyes closed.'

'Well, you'd expect that, wouldn't you, Ivan?' said a man who had come out with him.

Ivan turned to him.

'I don't know. When you see her on the Icon she's always got her eyes open. That's a good sign, isn't it? It means she's wide awake. You've got a chance. But with her just lying there –'

'It amounts to the same thing, though, doesn't it?'

'I'm not so sure. An icon's been blessed by the Church.'

'Well, the body will have been blessed too, won't it?'

'I don't know. I reckon it may not be the same thing. An icon's a bit special. Whereas a body, well, it is just a body, isn't it? And we've seen plenty of those.'

On their way to Yabloki Sad they passed Zapolonye. It consisted of about twenty mean houses and a small wooden church, where Sergei's father had, presumably, once officiated. It looked just an ordinary village.

Dmitri could not think why he had had the idea that it might not be.

Yabloki Sad looked a more prosperous place than Zapolonye. Not that that was saying much. The houses were still wooden and the road not made up, a mere track of frozen mud and ice. There were gardens in front of some of the houses, though, and willow trees bowed with snow.

The sleigh pulled up in front of one of these.

'It's me, Agafa!' cried Ivan.

'Well, bless my soul!' said a woman's voice within. 'And I thought it was Saint Nicholas!'

Some children came to the door, closely followed by the woman herself, wiping her hands on her apron.

'You've come in style, too,' she said.

'I've brought something, Agafa,' said the big man sheepishly.

He showed her the packages.

'The Barin's brought them from Kursk.'

'Well, blessings on Kursk, then,' said the woman. 'And on Your Honour.'

Ivan lifted them to the ground.

'Shall I bring them in?' he said.

'Ivan!' said the woman sternly.

'One of them?' he pleaded. 'Just one of them?'

'You take them to Simeon,' she directed. 'He'll divide them up.'

Ivan took a package in each hand and went along the street to one of the houses. An old man with a long grey beard was standing in the door.

'The Barin's brought some things for us,' said Ivan.

'Bring them in!'

'Simeon!' warned Ivan's wife, who had followed him along the street.

'I was going to divide them up,' the old man protested.

'Yes, well. Do it where we can all see.'

'There are some more in the sleigh,' said Ivan.

The old man's eyes widened.

'I'll have to call a meeting of the Mir,' he said.

'Oh, no!' said the driver. 'We'll be here for hours!'

Dmitri had heard about the village mir, as he had heard about zemstvos: distantly. The mir was the traditional village council, consisting of representatives of all the families of the village and attended by virtually everyone in the village. It was responsible for dividing out the village's land for the year, for the land was owned communally and worked by families according to custom and their need. It was also responsible for everything else that affected the village communally:

taxation, the church, the school if there was one. It was presided over by the starosta, a village elder; in this case, Simeon.

It took some time, as the driver had feared, for the people in the village to gather, partly because they walked so slowly, weakened through hunger and hardship, and even longer to get anywhere once they had arrived.

This was because they hadn't the faintest idea of procedure. The starosta had no notion about how to conduct a meeting but let people butt in, repeat themselves, introduce irrelevancies, lose track and generally wander as they chose. To Dmitri, who believed in meetings being short, businesslike and focused, it was a nightmare.

The packages, the inadequacy of which Dmitri was realizing more and more with every moment that passed, had been brought in and stood before them. For Dmitri, it would have been an easy matter, if that was what they wished, to divide them out. He would simply have taken the number of households and shared the contents of the packages out as equally as he could between them.

The Mir, though, did not find it quite so simple. What was 'household' for a start? Did households count equally? What about the number of mouths in each household? And then, when the packages were opened, what was 'equally?' Some goods were worth more than others and what they were worth was a matter for interminable argument. Dmitri could see that justice was being done, but it was being done, oh, so slowly!

If this was where, as the slavophils had it, the wisdom of the Russian people resided, Dmitri would almost have preferred the Zemstvo!

In the end, unable to bear it any longer, he slipped out. The driver followed and they made for the sleigh. Beside it, while they had been indoors at the meeting, another sleigh had drawn up. In it was Ludmilla Mitkin, the Governor's daughter, last seen in far away Kursk.

8

'I came to see for myself,' she said.

'I beg your pardon?'

'To see for myself. About the estate. You remember?' She looked at him. 'You must remember. We talked about it. You gave me advice. In the park.'

'About your family estate? Yes. I remember. But –'

'This is it.'

'Yabloki Sad?'

'Yes. It belonged to us once. The village and much else beside. All the land round here. Then we had to hand it over to the peasants, under the Tsar's reforms. And now, as I told you, Marputin wants to buy it back. And give it to me.'

'The village?'

'Yes. It was as you said. Ownership was vested in the community as a whole, which makes it much more difficult than if you were dealing with separate individuals. The whole Mir has to agree.'

'That'll take some doing!' said Dmitri feelingly.

'You think so? Marputin doesn't. He says things have changed. He thinks they could be willing to sell. But,' said Ludmilla passionately. 'I don't *want* them to sell. I want things to stay as they are.'

'Do you know why things have changed?' asked Dmitri. 'Why they might be willing to sell?'

'No?'

'Because they're starving, that's why.'

Ludmilla stood for a moment, stunned.

'I don't believe it! He couldn't be so –'

'There's famine all round here. Ordinary people are desperate.'

'And that's why they would be willing to sell?' she whispered. 'So that they could buy food?'

'That's right.'

'I came up here,' she said, 'to tell them – ask them – beg them not to sell! And now you're saying –?'

'I'm not sure I really am saying that.'

'What else can you be saying?' she demanded.

'I don't know. I really don't know.'

'It's so awful,' she said, her voice trembling. 'Whichever way. If they don't sell, they starve. If they do sell, I –'

She sat there for some time frowning in concentration.

Then, suddenly, she looked up.

'Dmitri Alexandrovich,' she said, 'what are you doing here?'

It was a question he found difficult to answer.

'I've been bringing some things over,' he prevaricated. 'A few parcels that friends at Kursk made up.'

'Food?'

'No. It would have been better if it had been.'

'Why don't I go into Tula tomorrow and get some?'

'It would cost money.'

'I've got money.'

'Not enough. You can't feed the whole village.'

'No?' said Ludmilla.

To his surprise, in the monastery yard next morning he saw Bibitkin.

'It ɔ my mother-in-law,' said the disgraced priest shamefacedly. 'She lives in Tula. The Blagochini says I've got to make my peace with her. Otherwise he won't be able to do anything for me.'

'What about that icon you sold?'

'The man's given it back.'

'Given it back?'

'Yes, he came into the church one morning and said that, on reflection, he had decided that he ought not to go ahead with the deal. Mindful of my suffering.'

96

'Oh, yes?'

'Yes. He said it had been no part of his intentions to bring calamity down upon the head of a poor, hard-working priest whose virtue was known to all the neighbourhood.'

'Oh, yes?'

'And so he was returning the icon.'

'He actually returned it?'

'Certainly.'

Dmitri could hear the edifice of his case cracking.

'It was the same man?'

'Yes.'

'And he brought the icon back?'

'Yes.'

'Did he ask you for the money?'

'Well, he did,' the priest admitted.

'And could you pay?'

'No, I explained that because of my difficult circumstances recently I had been obliged to lay out the money already on essentials.'

'And what did he say?'

'That he knew I was a man of my word and he would trust me to hand it back some time.'

'God almighty!'

'Moves in mysterious ways.'

Dmitri could not believe it. The case he had been building up so carefully, that he had begun to suppose was on the verge of getting somewhere, was suddenly in ruins.

'But, Barin,' said the priest worriedly, 'there lies the difficulty. I am a man of honour and I will repay him. Slowly, perhaps, rouble by rouble. Every month or two. Or perhaps every quarter. But I will repay. Once I get my job back.'

'Oh, I see.'

'Yes. And that depends, says the Blagochini, on me making peace with that old bitch. Which is likely to be one hell of a task, I can tell you. She's got me over a barrel, I'll have to pay her whatever she asks. And she knows it!'

'Can't you get your wife to say something to her?'

'I can't get my wife,' said the priest, 'to stop saying things to her!'

97

'Yes, well –'

'The thing is, Barin,' said Bibitkin confidentially. 'I need an advocate.'

'Yes, well you can forget about me.'

'But, Barin, you're just the man she would listen to. She respects real class. That's why she's never had any time for me. But a real Barin she'd go on her knees to.'

'But I'm not a real Barin,' objected Dmitri. 'I'm just a lawyer.'

'We don't have to tell her that. Go on, Your Excellency, be my saviour! Put in a word for me. Say old Bibitkin's not so bad. Tell her – tell her I might get promotion.'

'Well, that's not very likely, is it?'

'Say that I'm in with the Bishop. No, that won't do – she's in with the Bishop herself. Tell her – I know – tell her I've got friends at Court. The Consistory Court, that is.'

'So where is this unrest?' demanded Dmitri.

'Unrest?'

'There's a lot of unrest round Tula. According to the Corps of Gendarmes.'

'There's famine, certainly,' said the Father Superior.

'Unrest.'

'There have been marches,' conceded the Father Superior.

'Of whom?'

'Peasants, mostly. They've been the ones most affected, after all. Of course, everyone in an area where there is famine is affected in the end but the peasants are affected first because their income depends directly on the land and when the crop fails, the results are immediate. Whereas if you are in the town, working at a trade or in a factory, you'll be affected in the end but at the moment the money is still coming in. Especially in a place like Tula, where there are a lot of quite big factories – they make samovars and things like that – which sell primarily to other areas, areas which have not been hit by famine.'

'Where did they march?'

'To the Governor. To the Bishop. Asking for help.'

'Was there any violence?'

'Some. Not much. You've got to have strength for violence, and if you're not getting enough food, that's the thing that goes first.'

'I was out at Yabloki Sad yesterday. The people there seemed in a bad way.'

'Yes, that's one of the places most affected. All those villages over there. Zapolonye, Krebet –'

'Was that where the march started?'

'Some came from there. But, really, they came from all over the region. There was a rallying point outside the town and they all came together there.' The Father Superior hesitated. 'I think that may have been what called attention to it. That it was so near the town, I mean. Townspeople are always afraid that the peasants might turn on them. Merchants are afraid of their property being burned, that sort of thing. And it is true that there is a lot of feeling in the countryside against the town. People think that the merchants have stores of grain which they're hanging on to in the hope that prices will rise. And that, too, is true, I'm afraid.'

'But there's been no threat to the town as yet?'

'Not as yet. But people's memories are long. They remember that in the last century when there was famine, there was rioting. There were several notorious occasions when the peasants marched on Tula – once, they burned it down.'

'What about the Monastery?'

'They burned that down, too,' said the Father Superior cheerfully.

'But you've been all right this time?'

'Oh, yes. Business, as I told you, is booming. People are flocking in. The fact is, in Russia there's no one else to turn to. It's not much good looking to the authorities for help.'

'The Zemstvo?'

'Well, yes, perhaps,' said the Father Superior doubtfully. 'The Zemstvo.'

The Zemstvo was housed in a wooden building on Tula's main street. This was not an indication of distinction, since most of the buildings on the street were constructed of something more substantial. There was, however, a splendid brand new sign on the door which said Tula Zemstvo.

Dmitri knocked on the door and then, as no one paid any attention, went in.

There were several clerks, guards and officials, all too busy talking to be able to take much notice of visitors but opposite him the door to the main chamber room was open and through it he could see some of his packages lying on the floor.

He went in. Two men were bent over the packages opening them up, and round them Uncle Vlady was fluttering ineffectively. His face brightened when he saw Dmitri.

'Dmitri Alexandrovich!'

One of the men looked up.

'Kameron?' he said. He straightened up and shook hands. 'Vera Samsonova told me about you. I'm her counterpart here at the hospital.'

He introduced the other man, another doctor.

'The response has been amazing!' he said enthusiastically, gesturing at the packages filling the room, of which the Kursk consignment was only a small part.

'Everyone except the Government!' said the other man.

'Will you be able to use them?' asked Dmitri.

'Oh, yes. A lot of the stuff we'll have to sell. It would have been better if people had sold it at their end and just sent the money to us. And food. We're all right for food in Tula at the moment, though we soon won't be. The problem is getting it out to the villages.'

'Transport? Doesn't the Zemstvo have transport?'

The doctor looked at him.

'The Zemstvo doesn't have *anything*,' he said.

He met Ludmilla coming out of the bank.

'Credit,' she said, 'until they find out. But it means I can get started.'

And then he met Bibitkin, who fell upon him as on a long-lost brother.

'Barin!' he cried. 'Barin! You come at the moment of greatest need. Behold a man plunged in deepest despair!'

Dmitri beheld a man plunged in deepest vodka.

'A drop!' insisted Bibitkin. 'To carry me through the streets to the church, where I shall pray for the repose of that old bitch. And may it be soon!'

'You've spoken to your mother-in-law?'

'I would have,' said Bibitkin, 'if I'd got the chance. "Six roubles a month!" she shouted at me as soon as I got through the door. Six! "You must be mad!" I said. Or would have said if she hadn't caught hold of me by the neck and banged my head against the wall. "Six!" she shouted. "And not a kopeck less, you drunken old bastard!" Me, a man of religion! "My good woman," I said. And then she threw me out.'

'How much were you paying?' asked Dmitri.

'Three'

'You'll have to offer more.'

'Four?' said Bibitkin hopefully.

'Well –'

'Not that I can offer anything,' said Bibitkin despondently. 'While she's got this hold over me.'

'You'll have to do a deal.'

'How can I do a deal, Barin, if she won't even listen to me?'

'Talk to someone else. Her son-in-law, perhaps. Didn't you say she was staying with her other son-in-law?'

'I've got a better idea,' said Bibitkin. 'Why don't you talk to him?'

'That idle sod?' said the son-in-law. 'No chance! First, because if I did bring it up with her, she'd smash *my* head against the wall. Second, because –' he hesitated – 'the fact is, Barin, I'm not too keen on having her here myself. If he starts paying her more, I'll never get rid of her.'

'But, surely –?'

'Bibitkin's got it worked out,' said the son-in-law enviously. 'Three roubles a month to get rid of her! Cheap at the price. Wish I'd thought of it first.'

Dmitri considered.

'You could still do it,' he suggested.

'Bibitkin would never take her back.'

'He wouldn't have to. With you both paying, she could afford to live somewhere else.'

The son-in-law's eyes gleamed. Then the gleam faded. He shook his head regretfully.

'My wife would kill me,' he said. 'She's as bad as her mother.'

'However did you come to marry her? Bibitkin, I can understand. It all came with the job. But you –?'

'I got her in the grass once too often and then when they found she was pregnant, they wouldn't let go of me. You see, I've got a job at this factory, making samovars. It's a good job. The money's not too bad and it comes in regular. It was too good a chance for them to miss! No,' he said sadly, 'it's a nice idea but it won't do. If she learned I'd so much as suggested it –'

He stopped.

'Of course,' he said, 'if the suggestion came from someone else –'

'The thing is,' said Dmitri, 'while he's out of work, he can't even pay you the three roubles.'

The woman sniffed.

'He'd better agree to paying more, then.'

'So he should. But if you ask for too much, he won't be able to pay it – he won't be able to pay anything. And then where will you be?'

'Six roubles,' said the woman.

'Four.'

'Five roubles is my limit.'

'Four-and-a-half would be reasonable,' said Dmitri. 'Especially if you were getting some money from elsewhere.'

She looked at him quickly.

'Where would that money be coming from?'

'You could work the same trick with your other son-in-law. He's got a good job. He earns good money. He could afford four roubles a month.'

'Six,' said the old woman.

Dmitri sighed.

'You'd be taking it from your daughter.'

'She's a slut.'

'Very probably. But if you ask for six, he wouldn't agree.'

'He could pay more than four.'

'Why not ask for four and a half? Four and a half from them both. That would be nine roubles a month. Nine roubles!'

The woman wavered.

'If I asked for five, it would be ten.'

'It might be nothing. Remember, if Bibitkin's out of a job you don't get even the three roubles.'

'I suppose I could go and live with my sister,' she said slowly.

The following morning, when Dmitri came out into the Monastery yard, it was full of peasants; not beggars this time and even more definitely not pilgrims, but big, burly peasants, somewhat emaciated now, it was true, and many with faces haggard with hunger, but all intent on a conversation that was going on at the other end of the yard on the steps of the chapel.

'Out of the question!' the Father Superior was saying vehemently. 'Preposterous! Not to say barbarous!'

'But, Father,' an elderly man in front of him said quietly, 'times are hard. Something's got to be done.'

'I know times are hard! We're doing all we can, I've had an extra mass put on daily –'

'But, Father, that's general. What we want is something particular.'

'Yes, but to take a body and tramp all round the fields of Zapolonye –'

'But that's where it's needed, Father. That's where we want God's help. The crops were bad last year. If they're bad this year, we're done for.'

'Yes, but to take a body –'

'We wouldn't ordinarily, I know. We'd like an icon –'

'We *are* taking icons,' interrupted the Father Superior.

'Dozens of them. We'll take every icon in the place if that's what you want.'

'Yes, but, with respect, Father, it's not the same thing. These are not ordinary times and ordinary icons won't do. We need something special. Like the One-Legged Lady.'

'Yes, but you can't *have* the One-Legged Lady. First, because she's down in Kursk. And second, because she's not even there, she's been stolen.'

'We know that, Father. And that's why we want to use the body. I know it's not usual to carry a body in the Easter Procession but, as I say, times are hard. Things are getting desperate. We've got to do something. Otherwise people will start doing things they might regret.'

'Bodies are for graves,' said the Father Superior firmly. 'They are not for being carried all round the fields of Zapolonye in the Easter Procession.'

'I agree with you, Father. Bodies are for graves. Ordinarily. But this is no ordinary body. This is the One-Legged Lady. I don't reckon she'd mind. In fact, I reckon that when she sees the way things are, she'll be jumping out of her coffin!'

In the end, the Father Superior said he would think about it, and the peasants dispersed peacefully.

Dmitri, after reflection, drove into Tula, directing the sleigh to the Zemstvo building. As before, he found the two doctors bent over the parcels.

'Aren't there any more of you?' asked Dmitri.

'No one we can feel confident about,' said the doctors.

Looking at Uncle Vlady, fluttering his hands ineffectively on the periphery, Dmitri could see their point.

'You said you had a problem with distribution. I'm going out to Zapolonye. Can I take something?'

'Could you?' said the doctors gratefully.

'I'm always moving these bloody parcels about,' said the driver.

At first, Zapolonye seemed deserted. Thin curls of woodsmoke going up from the houses told him that it was not, but for a long time after the sleigh had stopped, not a door opened.

Eventually a man came out and stood in the doorway looking at them.

'I've brought some things.' said Dmitri.

'What for?' said the man.

'You can sell them,' said Dmitri, 'and buy food.'

'How much are the packages?'

'They're free.'

'Bollocks!' said the man. 'No one gives you anything for free.'

'These are free,' said Dmitri. 'They come from the Zemstvo.'

'What's the Zemstvo?'

Dmitri took a deep breath.

'It's in Tula. And it's sent these to help you.'

'We don't need help,' said the man.

'And we don't need anything from Tula,' said another voice.

Several men had come out.

'Who the hell are you?' one of them said.

'What are you doing here?' said another.

Dmitri was beginning to wonder.

'Let's get out of here,' muttered the driver.

One of the men came up to the sleigh and looked in at the packages.

'What are these, then?'

'They're for you,' said Dmitri.

The man shrugged and began to lift the packages out.

'Is it food?' said someone.

He tore open one of the packages and pulled out a silver fur muff that had belonged to Sonya.

'Bloody hell!'

'Are you taking the piss out of us?'

Some of the men came threateningly towards him.

'Barin! Barin!' cried a joyful voice suddenly.

It was Bibitkin.

He rushed up to Dmitri and embraced him.

'What the hell are you doing here?' asked Dmitri.

'I'm bringing her over. So that she can talk to her sister. She's agreed! Thanks to you! Oh, Barin, the relief, the joy, the pleasure!'

'Who the hell's this bloke?' said one of the men, astounded.

'He came over this morning. Bringing someone for Liza Proskova.'

'Did someone mention my name?'

For a moment Dmitri was under the impression that there were two mothers-in-law standing in the doorway.

One of them came across and looked at the packages.

'What this, then?'

She picked up the muff.

'It's from the Zemstvo,' said Dmitri. 'All these things are. You can sell them and buy food.'

'Oh, I like this!' said the woman, slipping her hands into the muff.

'Are there any more like that?' said the second mother-in-law, tearing open another of the packages.

'Get your hands off!'

'Don't talk to my sister like that!' shouted Liza Proskova.

'Her sister! Bloody hell, who would have believed there could be two of them!'

'She's coming to stay,' said Bibitkin, beaming.

'I'll have this,' said Liza Proskova, stuffing the muff up her apron.

'No, you won't!' shouted one of the men. 'You heard what the Barin said: it's got to be sold for food.'

'Share it out, then!' retorted Liza Proskova, 'I'll keep this.'

'It's worth twenty roubles!'

'You bloody put it back! The Mir will see to the selling. And to the sharing out.'

The women were driven off, protesting.

'What I don't understand,' said someone, 'is why this bloke should be giving us all this?'

'It's not me,' said Dmitri. 'It's from the Zemstvo.'

'What's that?' asked one of the men curiously. 'Something to do with the Monastery?'

'No, it's to do with the government.'

'It's not the Tsar?'

'The Tsar! You'll be lucky!'

'No, no, it's the local government.'

'The Governor?' said someone, puzzled.

'Not him either. It's – it's, well, it's like the Mir. Only for a bigger area.'

'Old Vlady Polikovsky and that lot?' said someone, better informed than the others.

'Well, I'm damned!'

The man began to gather up the packages.

'Brothers,' said an authoritative voice suddenly, 'ought we to be doing this?'

The men stopped.

'Doing what, Lev?'

'Accepting the stuff this man has brought.'

'Well, damn it, Lev, it's food, isn't it?'

'No, it's not. It's knick-knacks. We're being fobbed off with knick-knacks when what we need is food.'

'Well, yes, Lev, but –'

'Why haven't they sent us food?'

'You can sell –' began Dmitri.

The man disregarded him.

'You know why? Because all those rich merchants in Tula have got the grain locked up in their store-houses and they're not letting it out. And why is that? Because they're waiting for the prices to rise, that's why! They're waiting and we're starving! While all the time the grain is there.'

There were mutters of agreement.

'They could have sent us food. Instead, they sent us this!'

The man kicked one of the packages contemptuously.

'That won't feed us, brothers. Do you know why they have sent it? To fob us off. So that we won't go and get the grain for ourselves. Take what is rightfully ours.'

This time the murmurs were shouts.

'You've said it, Lev!' somebody called out.

The man pushed through the crowd and came up to Dmitri.

'So you can take this all back! And take yourself as well!'

'What's a rich man doing here, anyway?' cried someone. 'He's come here just to laugh at us!'

The crowd pressed angrily in on the sleigh.

The driver suddenly whipped the horses and tried to get

107

away. The sleigh started with a jolt but then slowed as the peasants got hold of it.

'Brothers!' cried Bibitkin desperately.

The sleigh came to a halt.

'What is all this?' said a deep voice suddenly.

Everyone looked up.

Coming out of the door of one of the houses was Ivan.

9

'Why, it's the young Barin!' he said, surprised. 'He's a friend of mine.'

'You pick funny friends, Ivan,' said Lev.

'I pick who I choose,' said Ivan, stepping out into the street.

Another man came out of the door behind him. It was the elderly man whom Dmitri had seen in the Monastery yard putting the peasants' case to the Father Superior.

'What is all this?' he said sternly.

The villagers fell back from the sleigh.

'The Barin was trying to help them,' said Bibitkin.

'I've brought some things,' said Dmitri, 'from the Zemstvo. You can sell them and buy food.'

'That's right,' agreed Ivan. 'He brought us some, too.'

'Knick-knacks,' said Lev contemptuously. 'To fob us off.'

'Food,' said Ivan. 'We've sold some already and bought grain. It didn't half come in handy, I can tell you.'

The elderly man looked at the contents of the packages that the two women had ripped open.

'Some of this is good quality staff,' he said. 'It would fetch a good price.'

'It's an insult,' said Lev.

'Give it to us, then,' said Ivan. 'We don't mind being insulted.'

'If it means food, Lev –' said someone uneasily.

'We'd do better to go to Tula and take it,' said Lev.

'I thought we'd agreed not to do that,' said the elderly man sharply.

'You may have agreed,' said Lev.

'The Mir agreed. Has it changed its mind? He looked round the crowd. 'We've got to do this properly. If you've changed your mind, well and good, but it's got to be done by the Mir properly. You can't decide you're going to do one thing and then go off and do another. We'll hold another meeting. If you like. But if you're not going to abide by the Mir's decisions, there's not much point in having one. And you'd better pick another starosta while you're at it.'

'Now, wait a minute, Panteleimon –'

'Hold on now –'

'We haven't changed our minds. Lev here was a bit ahead of things, that's all. We're still prepared to let the Old Lady have a go.'

'The Father Superior hasn't agreed yet,' said Lev.

'Even if he doesn't,' said Ivan, 'that needn't be the end of the story.'

'No,' put in Bibitkin, 'it needn't.'

'We said we'd wait,' said the starosta, 'and that's what we'll do.' He looked at the packages. 'And while we're waiting,' he said, 'these will keep us going.'

'Knick-knacks,' sneered Lev.

'They're food, Lev,' said one of the peasants quietly, 'and I can't afford to turn my back on food.'

The other villagers seemed to agree. They began to take the packages into one of the houses.

'They come from the Zemstvo, do they?' asked the starosta. 'Are they likely to be able to send us any more?'

'They've got a lot of stuff,' said Dmitri. 'It's coming from all over Russia. I brought some of this up from Kursk. The problem they've got is getting it out to the villages. And they're short-handed. You'd do better to go in and help them,' he said, looking at Lev, 'rather than causing trouble in Tula.'

'They won't want the likes of us,' said the *Starosta*.

'Maybe not,' said Dmitri, after a moment, 'but go in all the same. There are a couple of doctors there who are helpful. Tell them you're a *Starosta*.'

'We don't want charity,' said Lev.

'I want food,' said one of the villagers, looking up from

where he was picking up a package, 'and I don't care where it comes from.'

'You're right, though,' the starosta said to Lev, 'we don't want to be depending on charity. We want the crops to come good again. And that's where the One-Legged Lady comes in.'

'It's either that,' said Lev, 'or it's the journey to Opona.'

'Things passed off peacefully, did they?' said Volkov, when Dmitri got back to Kursk.

'I wouldn't say that,' said Dmitri.

'No?'

He told Volkov, in guarded terms, for he didn't want him to misconstrue what he, Dmitri, regarded as a fairly innocuous demonstration, what had happened at Zapolonye.

Volkov listened with great interest.

'And they were divided, you say, between those who wanted to wait for the One-Legged Lady and those who wanted to march immediately on Tula?'

'Not very immediately, I suspect,' said Dmitri. 'There were strong voices against.'

'But march?'

'They'd marched before,' said Dmitri unwillingly. He hadn't really intended to tell Volkov about this but he felt he had to say something, if only to justify what he regarded as the largely wasted time he had spent at Tula.

'They had?'

Volkov almost rubbed his hands.

'But dispersed peacefully.'

'This time,' said Volkov. He smiled his wintry smile. 'They haven't plucked up enough courage yet.'

Dmitri had awful visions of the Cossacks being sent in.

'I don't think we should make that kind of assumption,' he said quickly. 'There were, as I said, strong voices against.'

'Wanting them to wait for the One-Legged Lady?'

'Yes.'

He told Volkov about the confrontation in the Monastery yard.

'The Father Superior's not made up his mind,' he said.

111

'So if we act quickly there's time for us to influence his decision? Either way,' said Volkov, smiling.

'Of course, it would be barbaric to carry the body round the fields,' said Dmitri, 'but –'

'You think it would be better? But suppose it was carried round the fields? And suppose it didn't work? The crops stayed bad. Wouldn't that discredit the Church as well? And wouldn't that be worse?'

'Worse than what?' said Dmitri.

'Their marching on Tula,' said Volkov, smiling.

'I think it very important to encourage the peaceful voices,' said Dmitri.

Volkov just sat there smiling.

As the frightful possibilities began to dawn on Dmitri, he broke into a cold sweat.

He wished he had said nothing about the marches. He wished he had never gone to Tula.

'I really do not think that, at this moment, there would be any justification for anything other than peaceful measures!'

'Such as?' said Volkov.

'Well, the famine is the problem. Take away the starving and you take away the unrest.'

'Famine is something for the Church to bother itself with,' said Volkov detachedly. 'It's the unrest that concerns us.'

'With respect, the problem is so vast that the Church cannot be expected to handle it on its own.'

'I'm sure the Governor will be able to help.'

'As far as I could see, the only body actually doing anything was the local Zemstvo.'

'The Zemstvo?' said Volkov, surprised. He shrugged. 'Well, it's nice that it's found a job for itself. However, as I say, all that doesn't concern us. What does concern us is the evidence of potential unrest that you have so ably gathered.'

He considered for a moment.

'I don't suppose – there was no mention of Opona, was there?'

'A passing one, once.'

'What was it?'

Dmitri tried to remember.

112

'Something about, if the One-Legged Lady didn't work, the only thing left would be to try the journey to Opona.'

'They said that?'

'Yes, but, as I say, it was just a casual remark –'

'Casual? What,' said Volkov, 'do you think it meant?'

'Meant? Well, nothing much. If carrying the One-Legged Lady round the fields didn't work, then they'd be really up the creek, that's what I thought it meant.'

'Oh, no,' said Volkov. 'Oh, no. It meant something much more specific. Don't you see? The Kingdom of Opona is a kingdom without a king. It is a society in which there are no rulers, a society without government, a society which is truly anarchistic. It is an ideal that the peasants have always hankered after. And what they mean by the journey to Opona is setting out to create a society like that here! In place of the present one.'

Even in the few days that he had been away, Sonya's drawing room had filled up again. The floor was covered with old boots and shoes and items of clothing. Every surface – chairs, tables, foot-stools – contained some strange object: hats, umbrellas, tea-strainers, toilet-cases, china ornaments, musical boxes; and there in one corner was a samovar, similar to the ones he had seen at the Monastery.

'Boris Petrovich has been so kind,' said Sonya, following his glance. 'He absolutely insisted that we should have it. "There are those in greater need than I!" he said. I do think you have been unfair to him, Dmitri.'

'Yes,' said Igor Stepanovich, 'and he's collected a lot of money for us, too. More than some people I could mention.'

'I got him to collect it,' said Dmitri injured.

'You're good at getting other people to do the work,' said Vera Samsonova.

'As for the samovar . . .' said Dmitri.

They listened to his account of what had happened at the Monastery.

Vera shrugged.

'If it helps our cause –' she said.

'And, anyway,' said Sonya, 'I don't believe you. I'm sure he did it out of the kindness of his heart.'

Dmitri looked round at the piles of objects.

'You'd do much better to send them money, you know,' he said.

'Are you going to do some work sometime?' demanded Vera. 'Or are you just going to sit there and give us advice?'

'It's not me who says it. It's the Zemstvo. Not to mention the villagers.'

Sonya removed a feathered hat and boa from an armchair and sat down.

'It wouldn't be easy,' she said doubtfully.

'It would be easier for us than it is for them. You see, they have to sell it all down at their end and, of course, there isn't the money around, not with the famine, so it's hard to get a decent price.'

Vera sat back on her heels.

'That is a point,' she conceded.

Sonya's mother came in with tea for the workers. She looked despairingly round the room which had once been hers.

'There do seem a lot of things,' she said mildly. 'I had hoped –'

'Dmitri Alexandrovich says we ought to sell them,' said Sonya.

'Well, yes.' A gleam of hope came into her mother's eyes. 'That would seem a good idea.'

'But how?'

'Why not hold a bazaar, dear?'

She gathered up the glasses and went out.

'I suppose –' began Sonya.

'I don't think I'd be very good at bazaars,' said Vera Samsonova, with surprising humility.

'We *are* sending some money,' said Igor Stepanovich.

'Yes, but Dmitri is right. It would be much more helpful to them if we could sell the goods up here and just send them the money.'

There was a silence.

'A bazaar, then?' said Igor tentatively.

'Yes,' said Sonya, with sudden decision, 'a bazaar.'

'We'll need someone who knows something about it,' said Vera doubtfully.

'My mother,' said Sonya.

'Would she –?'

'Yes,' said Sonya firmly.

'We need someone else,' said Igor Stepanovich. 'We need a few important people on the committee.'

'Boris Petrovich?' suggested Dmitri.

'An opportunity,' Dmitri assured the Procurator, when they ran into each other that evening on their way into the Governor's house. 'You were looking for something that would convince the voters that you had a heart. This is it! A busy man like you making time for something as humble as this? Out of the goodness of your heart? Boris Petrovich, it will knock them over. Especially the ladies.'

The Procurator went on up the steps and inside. Dmitri hung back for a moment. Over beside the stables was the Governor's sleigh: and there beside it was the Governor's driver.

'Going out again?' asked Dmitri sympathetically.

'Early tomorrow. First thing I'm taking Miss Mitkin back to Tula. Why she wants to go to that God-forsaken hole, I can't think. It's even colder there than it is here.'

'It's a bit out of your usual way, isn't it? Mostly it's just the town and the Monastery, I imagine.'

'Monastery? We don't often go to the Monastery. His Excellency is not that holy!'

'Oh, sorry. I just noticed that you'd been there the other day and I thought maybe you were often there.'

'No, no. Once in a couple of months, something like that.'

'What was it I heard? You had an accident there or something?'

'A bloody fool of a woman. That old woman ought to be locked up,' I said to His Excellency. 'She's a hazard on the road.'

'She ought to have seen it was His Excellency and got out of the way.'

'She's a stubborn old bitch,' said the driver.

'Embarrassing for you. Especially when you had a passenger.'

'Well, that's it. What does he think? What sort of driver is that for a Governor, I'll bet he thinks? And, really, it wasn't my fault. It was that old bitch's!'

'A friend of the Governor's, was he?'

'No, not particularly. More a friend of Mr Marputin.'

'The Governor was just taking him out to see the Monastery, was he?'

'Yes. Mostly the icons, I think. He went into the Chapel while His Excellency was off inside, talking to the Father Superior.'

'Down here often?'

'From time to time. Usually when Marputin is staying.'

Volkov's sleigh came into the yard and Dmitri went into the house with him. He suspected that it was owing to his association with Volkov that he had been invited this evening. Assistant Procurators did not normally figure on Governor's invitation lists.

He remembered his last visit. Not unless they wanted something.

'Dmitri Alexandrovich!' cooed the Governor's wife. 'How good to see you. I gather you have been helping Mr Volkov?'

'A little,' said Dmitri.

'A lot,' said Volkov.

'That explains why we have not seen much of you lately.'

'I have had the advantage of you, Maman,' said Ludmilla, 'for I have seen Dmitri Alexandrovich very recently. In Tula.'

'Tula?' said Volkov.

'My family has an estate there,' said the Governor's wife.

'Really?' said Volkov.

'Yes. And Ludmilla has been going up to see it. We have hopes –'

'Is that wise?' asked Volkov.

116

'Wise?'

'At this time?'

'I gather from Ludmilla that there is famine in the region, but –'

'Unrest,' said Volkov. 'Peasant unrest.'

'I wouldn't go so far –' began Dmitri.

The Governor cut in.

'You don't think it may be dangerous for Ludmilla, do you?' he said to Volkov.

'Mr Kameron found it so.'

'Really?'

The Governor looked thoughtful.

'Perhaps you'd better not go again, my dear,' he said to Ludmilla.

'I have already made arrangements,' said Ludmilla.

'Yes, but –'

'There's no risk of it, well, of it spreading up here?' asked the Procurator anxiously.

'You're the ones who should be telling me that,' said Volkov.

'No,' said Dmitri.

'You're very sure,' said Volkov, 'and yet you, yourself, again, witnessed an episode out at the Monastery –'

'That was nothing,' said Dmitri.

'I hope so,' said Volkov.

'Your Excellency, I can assure you we shall do everything we can –' said the Governor, sweating.

'My goodness, yes,' said Boris Petrovich.

They went into dinner, Ludmilla on Dmitri's arm. If he owed this elevation, too, to his association with Volkov, Dmitri was beginning to think that there was something to be said for the Corps of Gendarmes.

'You weren't hurt?' asked Ludmilla.

'No.'

Dmitri hesitated.

'All the same,' he said, 'I think your father might have a point. Just at the moment.'

Ludmilla shook her head firmly.

'It's all arranged,' she said. 'I've got to go.'

'What's arranged?'

'I've tricked Marputin.'

'Listen, Ludmilla, nice people often think they can trick nasty people, but –'

'I've got him to make an advance to the villagers. On account, as it were.'

'He's lending them money?'

She nodded.

'They'll drink it all,' said Dmitri. 'Don't you see? Then they'll be back where they started. Only worse off.'

Ludmilla's eyes widened.

'More in his hands than ever?'

'That's right.'

Ludmilla considered; then made up her mind.

'I'll get him to lend the money in the form of credit; with me. And I will only give them food.'

Dmitri was silenced. He was never very good with money and tried to think about it as little as he could. Anything involving money that was the least bit complex was beyond him. Ludmilla seemed able to think about such matters on her feet: he couldn't.

Not on money, that was. On other things, however –

'Ludmilla,' he said, 'Marputin wouldn't have done this unless you had promised him something.'

'I promised him nothing.'

'Are you sure?'

'I might have led him to believe I was promising him something,' she conceded.

'Ludmilla –'

'I know what I'm doing,' she said.

Far off across the snow they could see the sparkle of the gold onion; and there, as before, was the black smudge of pilgrims, only this time it was not a blot in front of the Monastery gates but a black piece of crepe, with one end fastened to the Monastery entrance and the other stretching back along the road.

'They're still coming,' said Dmitri.

Volkov had set off for the Kursk Monastery the next morning and had told Dmitri he was coming with him.

'I've got things to do here,' Dmitri had protested. 'The Icon –'

But Volkov had insisted and that was that. Now he looked over the side of the sleigh at the marching pilgrims.

'And going,' he said.

He ordered the driver to stop, got out of the sleigh and walked over to some of the pilgrims who were leaving the Monastery.

'Where are you going?' he asked.

'Tula, Your Excellency,' said the pilgrim, surprised.

Satisfied, Volkov got back into the sleigh.

They went on for some way in silence, until, in fact, they were beginning to pick out the other vegetables and fruit on the Monastery roof.

'Why did it start here?' asked Volkov suddenly.

'I don't think it did start here,' objected Dmitri. 'It started in Tula with the failure of the crops and –'

'It started with the theft of the Icon,' said Volkov. 'That was the first actual action.'

'There were marches –'

But Volkov was not listening.

'The famine created the necessary conditions,' he said, 'but for it to move from passive to active something else was required: a focus for the unrest, something behind which they could marshal.' He looked at Dmitri, 'The One-Legged Lady,' he said.

'If that was so,' said Dmitri, 'why hasn't she appeared at Tula?'

'I have been asking myself that. And the answer that I have come to is that she is intended to be used not up there but back here.'

'An uprising? Here?' said Dmitri incredulously.

Volkov nodded.

'But there is no sign of that! It's quite –'

Dmitri was going to say loony but thought better of it.

– 'impossible,' he finished.

'I think I got here at the right time,' said Volkov. 'Early.'

As they approached the Monastery gates the sleigh had to slow down because there were so many pilgrims.

'Still coming from Tula,' said Volkov, 'and still going back to Tula. There is obviously a link; and I mean to find him.'

In his previous interrogation of the monks Volkov had identified all those with Tula connections. Now he interviewed them again, this time with Dmitri sitting beside him. Dmitri was not at all happy about that. Firstly, because he did not like being associated so openly and clearly with the Corps of Gendarmes, both for personal reasons and public ones – he believed that the law must establish itself as completely independent of the Government and the Government's agencies. Secondly, he did not accept for one moment Volkov's analysis of the situation. He saw no sign of an uprising, certainly not down here. The traffic between Tula and here, which Volkov saw as suspicious, Dmitri saw as understandable given the famine in Tula and the belief they had in the miraculous workings of the Icon. What he feared now was that Volkov would alight on some unfortunate individual and establish his part in a conspiracy which, in Dmitri's, view, almost certainly did not exist.

Among the monks whom Volkov interviewed again was, naturally, Father Sergei. He made no secret of his Tula connections.

'Why should I? Everyone knows I was born there. Everyone knows I went to the Kaminski. It was the natural thing to do for anyone who lived up there.'

'And what did you learn at the Kaminski?' asked Volkov.

'The spiritual exercises. Spiritual discipline.'

'Anything else?'

'Like what?' asked Father Sergei.

'Undesirable social sympathies.'

'For whom?'

'The peasants.'

'I didn't learn them,' said Father Sergei. 'I had them. I was a peasant.'

This was the wrong thing to say. In Old Russia every individual's rank had been prescribed; and although the system had weakened, the difference between social groups was still felt strongly. The clergy were to some extent a caste, marrying among themselves and bringing up their children to follow in their footsteps – of which, of course, Father Sergei himself was an example. To live among peasants was one thing; to describe oneself as one was quite another. It raised Volkov's eyebrows.

'And these social sympathies,' he said, 'you took them with you into the Kaminski?'

'Naturally.'

'Where they were able to find expression?'

'In religious form. Only in religious form,' said Father Sergei pointedly.

Volkov asked him if he was still in contact with people in the area. Father Sergei hesitated slightly. Dmitri knew why.

He would be asked for their names.

'My family, naturally.'

'You see them often?'

'Often? Hardly ever.'

'But you send messages to them, perhaps?'

'Perhaps.'

'Frequently?'

'On Feast Days.'

'Other people? Friends?'

'I've lost touch,' said Father Sergei.

With the other monks it went much the same. Nearly all came from families with some Church connection and most from the villages around Tula. It had been natural for them to go to the Kaminski, the main monastery in the area. And once they had entered upon the religious life, they had tended to lose contact with what they had left behind them. A few still had relatives in the area with whom they were occasionally in touch. They exchanged greetings at Christmas, were sent pascha cheeses at Easter.

Few of them were educated men. Hardly any merchants sent their sons into the Church, and no noblemen did. There was no tradition in Russia, as there was in other European countries, of the gentry sending younger sons into the Church. People like the Father Superior were an exception.

Volkov might raise his eyebrows at Father Sergei's admission that he was a peasant, but that was what they were. It was even more true of the village priests; and Dmitri could suddenly see how someone like Bibitkin, with all his faults, might be more genuinely acceptable to the villagers that someone more cultivated. Father Sergei was no Bibitkin; but Dmitri could see now where his easy familiarity with the pilgrims came from. He could see, too, why a man like Father Sergei, while he might lack sympathy for and even acquaintance with the radical ideas that were circulating in the big cities of Russia, the St Petersburgs and the Moscows, might nevertheless have considerable fellow-feeling for those suffering at the present time in the villages around his birth-place.

But sympathy for was a very different thing from action on behalf of.

'Is it?' said Volkov. 'Doesn't action arise out of sympathy?'

They still hadn't finished their interviews when Volkov broke off for the day. Dmitri was glad of the chance to continue with his own investigation. He went round to the woodshed at the back of the Monastery. As he opened the door, the sweet, heavy fragrance of the pine rushed out and hit him.

At the far end of the shed, beside the big store in which wet logs were hissing and spitting, were Peter Karpov and his friend the carter. They were seated on packing cases, with large mugs of kvass in their hands.

'Why, it's the young Barin!' said Peter, rising.

'Can I join you?'

The carpenter pulled up another case; then hesitated.

'Yes, please,' said Dmitri.

The carter filled him a glass.

'I've seen your friend,' said Dmitri, taking a sip, 'Bibitkin.'

'Oh, yes?'

'Yes. At Tula.'

'At Tula, then?'

'Yes. Things are working out better for him. I spoke to the mother-in-law. She's prepared to agree.'

The carpenter seemed to relax.

'Well, that's good,' he said.

'Bibitkin's all right,' said the carter. He pushed his case back to give Dmitri more room. His back was almost touching the contraption the carpenter had made to help carry the One-Legged Lady.

'You've got it mended, then?'

'Mended?'

Dmitri indicated the contraption.

'Oh, yes. Taking it back soon.'

'We've not found the One-Legged Lady, though.'

'No.'

Dmitri drank deep; then chose his moment.

'Tell me,' he said, 'why did you cut the chains?'

'Why did I cut the chains?'

'Yes. The ones holding the Old Lady.'

Peter looked at the carter.

'Because you was told to,' offered the carter. Dmitri wasn't sure whether it was a question or a statement.

'Because I was told to.'

'Who by?'

The carpenter sat silent.

'Who by?'

'I don't remember,' said the carpenter. 'It was a long time ago.'

'Not very long.'

'I don't recall.'

'Try.'

'The Father Superior?' suggested the carter.

'Yes,' said the carpenter, 'the Father Superior.'

When Dmitri went out into the yard the next morning he found Volkov standing by the gates watching the endless line of pilgrims.

'Any of them,' he said, turning to Dmitri. 'Any of them could be taking messages.'

They went back to interrogating. A surprising number of the monks, Dmitri was obliged to admit, seemed to have come from Tula.

'Coincidence?' said Volkov dryly.

This morning he was concerned to ascertain whether any of them had visited Tula recently. One or two of them had. To visit sick or dying relatives they said. And, more difficult, had any of them been visited?

'People are always sticking their hands in at the kitchen,' said Father Osip, rubbing his chin.

Volkov noted this down, as he did the names of the monks who had visited Tula recently.

'First the desire and then the opportunity,' he said. 'Some of them have more opportunities than others. But we shall have to check up on them all.'

Dmitri didn't like the sound of this. Volkov had said 'we' but Dmitri suspected that it wasn't going to be Volkov who was doing most of the work.

When they got back to Kursk the next day Maximov was waiting for them on the steps of the court-house. He rushed down to meet them.

'Your Excellency. Your Excellency!' he cried. 'Something has just come in!'

He paused self-importantly.

'Well?' said Volkov.

'The One-Legged Lady has come back!'

10

For a moment Dmitri thought that it was the Icon that had returned, in the way that Bibitkin's had.

'No, no,' said Maximov. 'The real One-Legged Lady.'

'The real One-Legged Lady?'

'The – the person.'

'Bollocks!' said Volkov.

It was unlike him to express himself so crudely. He liked to maintain always an icy composure. But it was difficult to maintain icy composure when bodies were rising from their graves.

'Where does this report come from?' he snapped.

'The Chief of Police at Tula.'

Maximov produced an envelope. As he was tearing it open, Volkov stopped.

'How did you know what was inside?' he demanded.

'Timofei told me.'

'Who's Timofei?'

'The driver, Your Excellency.'

'Fetch him.'

They were all in the Procurator's office. Maximov went out and returned with a quaking police driver.

'How did you know what was inside this?'

He showed him the letter.

'Everyone knows it, Your Excellency. It's all over Tula.'

'What, exactly, is all over Tula?'

'That the One-Legged Lady has risen from the grave.'

Volkov snorted.

'And what is she doing?' asked Dmitri.

'What she did before. Going round and giving food to people.'

'Causing trouble?' asked Volkov.

'She's giving food,' said the driver uneasily.

'Are the people coming to her?'

'Oh yes.'

Volkov crumpled the letter in his hand.

'Shall I get the Cossacks in, Your Excellency?' asked Maximov.

Volkov thought for a moment.

'We've got them standing by, haven't we?'

'Yes, Your Excellency. The other side of Kursk.'

Volkov came to a decision.

'Transfer them to Tula. I'll give you a note.'

'But, Your Excellency –' began Boris Petrovich, worried.

'Yes?'

'Suppose there's trouble here? And the Cossacks are up in Tula?'

'You'll just have to deal with it yourself, won't you?'

'Yes, Your Excellency. Of course, Your Excellency.'

The Procurator sounded even more worried.

'There won't be any trouble!' said Dmitri.

Volkov looked at him.

'Not here, no,' he agreed. 'Tula is where it's beginning to happen. I thought it would be here.'

'Well, good luck,' said Dmitri.

'You're coming with me,' said Volkov.

Dmitri ran to his lodgings to get a change of clothing. On his way back he met Sonya.

'Tula?' she said. 'You don't think you could take –?'

'No, I bloody don't!' said Dmitri. 'I'm going with Volkov.'

Sonya hurried along beside him.

'Perhaps some money?' she said. 'We've got some now that Boris Petrovich is being so successful at securing contributions.'

'Look, I can't wait –'

But Sonya had dashed off. She returned again just as they were getting into the sleigh and thrust a large envelope at him. Dmitri stuffed it unwillingly into his furs.

On the way they called in briefly at the Monastery. Volkov

126

went in to see the Father Superior. Dmitri stamped up and down outside in the snow trying to get some circulation going. He became aware that Father Kiril was watching him from the door of the Chapel.

'Where are you going to?'

'Tula.'

'Yes,' said Father Kiril. 'That's where she came from and it's to there that she'll be returning. The apple doesn't fall far from the tree, does it?'

Volkov returned, accompanied by the Father Superior. Father Kiril vanished into the Chapel. As Volkov went round to the other side of the sleigh and began to climb in, Father Osip came rushing out of the kitchen and gave the driver a small bag.

'You take that for me, will you, my son?' he said. 'Just hand it to the monk in the Kaminski gate-house.'

The sleigh sped through the Kaminski gates. The Father Superior must have seen them coming for he was already waiting in the yard. Volkov jumped out.

'Don't bother to tell me what happened,' he ordered. 'Just tell me where she is now.'

'She?' said the Father Superior, surprised.

'The One-Legged Lady.'

'Where she was, I hope,' said the Father Superior. 'In her coffin.'

'In her coffin?' said Volkov. 'But –?'

'There's a crazy rumour that the One-Legged Lady has come back,' said Dmitri.

'Ah, yes,' said the Father Superior, 'but that's no rumour.'

'What do you mean?' said Volkov. 'I thought you said she was in her coffin?'

'*Our* One-Legged Lady is; this is another one.'

'An impostor? They've gone that far? Things have started to move,' he said to Dmitri.

'Where is she?' he asked the Father Superior. 'This new One-Legged Lady?'

'Where the old one originally came from,' said the Father Superior. 'Yabloki Sad.'

'Yabloki Sad?' said Dmitri.

They picked up some policemen in Tula. The sleighs travelled together in an uneasy convoy. All the policemen were armed.

When they came to Yabloki Sad they found the single street empty but soon people began to appear in the doorways. They just stood in the doorways looking at the policemen and did not come any closer.

'You!' said Volkov, beckoning to one of the men.

Reluctantly the man came forward.

'Where's the *Starosta?*'

The man pointed to one of the houses. A man came out of it and walked towards them. It was the man who had taken charge of dividing out the parcels the other day, Simeon.

'Are you the *Starosta* of this village?'

'Yes, Your Excellency.'

'Have you a woman here?'

'Woman, Your Excellency?'

'The One-Legged Lady?'

The *Starosta* shook his head.

One of the policemen pointed up the street to where a sleigh stood outside one of the houses.

Volkov climbed out of his sleigh. Dmitri saw suddenly that he had a revolver in his hand. The police fanned out around him.

The people in the doorways had gone very quiet.

Volkov went up to the house and threw the door open.

'Why, hello!' said Ludmilla, surprised.

'What the hell do you think you're doing here?' snapped Volkov, when he had recovered.

'I live here,' said Ludmilla.

'Not here, you don't!' said Volkov, looking around him.

It was an ordinary single-room peasant's hut, with a brick stove on which someone was lying. There were some homemade wooden chairs and a table, and along one wall a crude dresser on which pots and pans were stacked.

Otherwise there was practically nothing, a few blankets,

perhaps, and some clothes; big peasant boots beside the door, some smaller ones, children's, beside the stove, drying out. There, too, were some clogs made out of birch-bark, belonging to a woman. There were no windows. What light there was came through a hole in the roof which served as a chimney; ineffectively, since the room was thick with smoke.

'Nearby,' said Ludmilla. 'It's our estate.'

'Your estate?' said Volkov.

'Or was,' said Ludmilla.

Dmitri could see now that she had brought some baskets with her. They were full of food: bread, root vegetables, some grain.

The bundle on the stove stirred.

'Who's that?' said an old, quavery voice.

'Just someone come to visit,' said Ludmilla.

'Has he brought anything?'

Volkov retreated outside, fuming. Ludmilla followed him out.

'You ought not to be here,' he said.

'Oh?' said Ludmilla. 'Why not?'

'Because it's dangerous. I thought you understood that. I thought that when we were at your father's, it was agreed –'

'I had made arrangements,' said Ludmilla.

'To come here?'

'To visit our estate. To see for myself.'

'Well, now you've seen,' said Volkov, 'perhaps you'd better go straight back home.'

'On the other hand,' said Ludmilla, 'now that I've seen, perhaps I had better not.'

Volkov's eyes became ice.

'You've caused enough trouble already!' he said.

'I am not aware of having caused any trouble,' said Ludmilla.

'There was a report that the One-Legged Lady had returned,' said Dmitri. 'It seems that you are it.'

Ludmilla laughed.

'It's no laughing matter, young lady,' warned Volkov. 'The Corps of Gendarmes does not like being made a fool of.'

'It seems to me,' said Ludmilla, 'that in this case it has made a fool of itself.'

Volkov hovered there uncertainly for a moment and then stamped off.

Dmitri put his hand in his pocket and pulled out the envelope Sonya had entrusted to him.

'From some well-wishers at Kursk,' he said, pushing it towards her.

Then he followed Volkov.

Further along the street, the police were climbing back into the sleighs. The villagers had come out of their doorways and were gathered now in a silent, hostile crowd. Dmitri saw Ivan looking at him with a puzzled expression on his face.

Volkov beckoned the Chief of Police.

'But, Your Excellency,' wailed the Chief of Police, 'there were reports –'

'Don't you ever check reports?'

'Always, Your Excellency. Always! But this time –'

'You thought you'd make a fool of the Corps of Gendarmes!'

'No. Your Excellency, no! It was so urgent! I thought you needed to know. At once!'

'Well, there's something in that.' Volkov conceded. 'However –'

'The countryside is up in arms, Your Excellency! There was a march. Only last week!'

'Yes,' said Volkov, looking at Dmitri. 'I heard about that.'

'And there's talk of another one.'

'There is?'

'Yes, Your Excellency,' said the Chief of Police in relief, seeing his opportunity. 'All the villages are full of it. Zapolonye, Gorge, Holm –'

'You should have sent me a report on that,' said Volkov. 'Not on all this nonsense about the One-Legged Lady.'

'But. Your Excellency, that's part of it. They say she's coming back –'

'I'm warning you!'

'But, Your Excellency,' wailed the Chief of Police, almost in tears. 'They do!'

'They're hoping the Father Superior is going to allow them to carry the One-Legged Lady's corpse around the fields,' said Dmitri. 'That's all it is.'

'That's right, Your Excellency, I mean, that's wrong, Your Excellency. That was what they were hoping. But now, now they're saying something different. They say no, she's going to come back of her own accord –'

'Bollocks!' said Volkov.

'I know. Your Excellency. Of course it's bollocks. But – but that's what they're saying, Your Excellency. She's going to come back and lead them –'

'Lead them?' said Volkov.

'That's what they're saying, Your Excellency. Lead them – there's talk of another march. On Tula. Only it won't end so peacefully this time. That's what they're saying, Your Excellency. This time it's going to be bread or burn.'

'Bread or burn?' said Volkov. 'Is that what they are saying?'

'Zapolonye,' said Volkov, as they went past it. 'Wasn't that one of the villages he mentioned? Where there was trouble? And wasn't that where you –?'

'Yes,' said Dmitri, 'but I wouldn't say –'

But Volkov wasn't listening.

'And wasn't that where one of those monks came from?'

'Father Sergei,' said Volkov, coming to the next name on his list.

They had turned into the Kaminski Monastery and he had gone straight to the Father Superior, where he had taken from his pocket a list of all the monks at the Kursk Monastery who had Tula connections. He was going through them one by one.

'Ah, Father Sergei,' said the Father Superior, shaking his head.

'You know him?'

'I remember him only too well. It blew up at just about the time I came to the Monastery. It was my first unpleasant duty. I think my predecessor had seen what was coming and decided that this was the time to step down. And leave it to me!'

'What did he leave to you?'

'The trial. Well, it wasn't quite that, we don't go in for that sort of thing. Call it – well, a difficult interview. After which Father Sergei left the Monastery and went to Kursk.'

'What had he done?

The Father Superior hesitated.

'It wasn't any one particular thing. Just, let us say, demeanour that was inappropriate.'

'Towards whom?'

'My predecessor, for a start. He thought him an interfering old fool. Well, you know – but he shouldn't have said so!'

'What did he disagree with him about?'

'Blight.'

'Blight?'

'It was a bad year for the crops that year. The blight was spreading and the Governor ordered the whole crop burnt. To prevent it affecting neighbouring areas, you know. Well, it was a perfectly sensible measure and Father Sergei was prepared to accept it. But then he wanted compensation for the villages whose crops had been burnt.'

'What was it to do with him?' said Volkov, astonished.

'That's what the Governor said. And that was the next occasion on which Sergei showed inappropriate demeanour. Grossly inappropriate I mean; he had always been difficult. "Compensation," said the Governor. "You'll be asking for golden elephants next!" "They'll die," said Father Sergei. "Well, get some subscription up!" said the Governor. "Get the Monastery to do it. That's what monasteries are for!"'

The Father Superior looked at Volkov.

'I am afraid that the Governor, the previous Governor, that is, not the present one, had an imperfect idea of the spiritual functions of institutions such as ours.'

'Get on with it,' said Volkov.

'Well, then Father Sergei went to my predecessor and asked what the Kaminski was going to do. "Offer up prayers," said my predecessor. "Yes," said Father Sergei, "but what are we going to *do*?"'

The Father Superior looked at them again apologetically.

'I am afraid that Father Sergei, too, showed an imperfect understanding of what monasteries are about. Which is, of course, much more serious in a priest than in a Governor. As my predecessor told him.' The Father Superior paused. 'That was the second occasion on which Father Sergei showed inappropriate demeanour. What was worse, he took no notice.'

'Took no notice?' said Volkov.

'He began to organize the distribution of Monastery stores to the villages affected. Well, of course, that was all very well. Up to a point. But when it began to affect the Monastery's own meals, some of the monks began to complain. "We're used to fasting," Father Sergei said. "It will do us no harm." But that was not how the other monks saw it. The older ones, at least. Some of the younger ones sided with Father Sergei.'

'Ah!' said Volkov.

'Yes. A split developed between the younger monks, led by Father Sergei, and the older ones. This was bad for the Monastery, very bad, and some of the older monks remonstrated with him.' The Father Superior paused again. 'That was the third time,' he said, 'that Father Sergei showed inappropriate demeanour.'

'Lack of respect,' offered Volkov.

'Indeed. Of course, he was young. And very close to the peasants. His father had been priest over at – where was it? – Zapolonye.'

Volkov sat back, pleased.

'Not only a rebel,' he said, 'but a leader!'

'It was years ago!' protested Dmitri.

'Once a rebel, always a rebel,' said Volkov. 'That sort of thing shows itself early.'

'You'll need more than that to convince a court,' said Dmitri.

'I wasn't thinking of bringing him before a court,' said Volkov carelessly.

Dmitri knew what that meant. He would be treated as a

'political' prisoner. That is, he would be brought not before an ordinary court but before an Administrative Tribunal of the Ministry of the Interior, where the rules were not at all the same. There would be no jury, no legal counsel to defend him. The rules of proof would not be as stringent. All that was required was that the Tribunal should be persuaded that the person brought before it was a potential threat to the State.

A tide of anger rose within him. This was exactly the kind of thing which as a constitutional lawyer he was fighting against.

'Even an Administrative Tribunal,' he said, 'will require something more than this.'

'Once you have the man,' said Volkov detachedly, 'you soon find what you want.'

'Even if it isn't there? There isn't a single thing to connect him with present disaffection –'

He stopped. Because he suddenly realized that there was.

As soon as he could get away, he went out into the yard and across to the gate-house. The monk inside looked up.

'Our driver was bringing you a bag, said Dmitri. 'I think it was from Father Osip. Or was it Father Sergei?'

'Father Osip, this time,' replied the monk.

'Has it been collected yet?'

'Not yet. Someone will probably came in from Zapolonye tomorrow on the log-cart. It's usually Father Sergei's cousin. If there's something for Father Osip's people he drops it off on the way back.'

'Father Osip comes from Zapolonye too?'

'Near there. They grew up together.'

So the bag was still there, and with it the evidence that Volkov needed of the link between Father Sergei and the 'rebellion' around Tula; for, once the existence of the covert postal service had been revealed, Volkov would very soon establish that other people beside Father Osip had been using it to send messages. Should Dmitri tell him?

He shrank back. The bag probably contained nothing but harmless letters to Father Osip's relatives but even that was enough to damn him. Mere association with rebels was enough to send a person to Siberia; and the relatives might well, especially with a stretch of Volkov's imagination, fall into that category.

There was another consideration too. Once the existence of the postal service had been revealed to Volkov, he would be in a position to intercept letters; and whereas Father Osip's letters might well be innocuous, Father Sergei's might not be. From what the Father Superior had said, Father Sergei was just the chap to say something out of turn, especially if he was writing to relations or friends whom he knew to be starving. Telling Volkov might send two innocent people into exile.

But that supposed that the letters they were sending were innocent. Suppose they were not?

Well, that was Volkov's concern, not his. At least, until there was definite evidence to suggest that a crime had been committed or was likely to be committed. That was the difference between Volkov and him, between the Corps of Gendarmes and the independent legal system that Dmitri was fighting to create. He could settle the matter by opening the bag but it was for Volkov to open people's correspondence merely on vague suspicion not for him. He wouldn't do Volkov's dirty work.

He decided that, for the time being at least, he would keep his discovery to himself.

The next morning Volkov went off to Tula to talk to the Chief of Police about the peasants' marches. Dmitri stayed behind at the Monastery. He had had enough of being too publicly associated with the Corps of Gendarmes.

He was just crossing the yard on his way back from breakfast when he saw the gates being opened to let Volkov's sleigh out. At once, a huge crowd of peasants surged in and made straight for the kitchens. Within minutes a long queue was stretching back almost to the gates. Dmitri went to see what was going on.

He found that the monks were serving kasha, oatmeal porridge, to everyone. At lunch, one of the monks told him, they served shchee, cabbage soup. Shchee da kasha, peescha nasha, ran the traditional peasant song. Cabbage soup and oatmeal porridge is our food. And that was about all it was in times of shortage.

But at least it was something. And at this stage in the famine, after so many months, and with their stores depleted, it was the best, the monk explained, that the Monastery could do. At any rate it kept people alive. Just.

The line of people stretched out now through the gates. A log-cart was having difficulty coming in. There were several men sitting on top of it. One of them seemed vaguely familiar. Dmitri looked again. It was Bibitkin. Of course! It must be the log-cart from Zapolonye that the monk in the gate-house had spoken about. Yes, and to confirm it, one of the men jumped down, ran into the gate-house and re-emerged with the bag Father Osip had sent. That, no doubt, was Father Sergei's cousin. He climbed back up on to the log-cart and it continued on its way round to the back of the building.

Some time later he saw Bibitkin again. He was working his way along the line.

He smiled when he saw Dmitri.

'Just raising some roubles,' he said, 'so that I can get back to Kursk.'

He turned back to the line.

'What about it, then? I do weddings, funerals, baptisms – Just think of the little ones! How will they go to heaven if they've not been baptised? And it could happen at any minute! What with all this hardship, the poor little ones are dying like flies. That little one, for instance –'

He stopped opposite a woman holding a baby.

'Who knows what could happen? It would lie heavily on you, Mother, if he –'

'She,' said the woman.

'– were to go even before you got back to the village. Think of the child! Are you going to cast away his –'

'Her.'

'– chances of salvation?'

'We haven't got any money.'

'A few kopecks. Only a few kopecks! I've brought down my charges. Times are hard for all of us.'

'We've got our own priest,' said the man beside her. 'We'll have it done at the village.'

'Ah, but suppose you don't get back to the villages in time? It's a cold day, and –'

'We haven't money for the likes of you,' the man said shortly.

'But I'll do it for less. You'll save. Whatever he charges, I'll go lower. Three-quarters, now; there's an offer! Half!'

The woman looked at the man doubtfully.

'We could buy food with the difference, couldn't we?'

'We could buy even more if we didn't have it done at all!'

'Oh!' cried Bibitkin, appealing to the queue. 'Do you hear that? A man throwing away his child's hope of eternal life just to save a kopeck!'

'You shut up!' said the man.

'Oh, the hardness of his heart!' cried Bibitkin, skipping back nimbly out of reach. 'Brother, I will pray for you.'

He dropped on his knees.

'Forgive him his sin –'

'Look, just go away!' said the man.

'– the hardness of his heart –'

'Will you go away?' said the man desperately.

'That will be a kopeck,' said Bibitkin, rising to his feet.

'A kopeck? What for?'

'Prayers cost a kopeck. Though one prayer won't do much for a man like you. Perhaps another –?'

He dropped on his knees again.

'All right, all right!'

The man fished in his pocket and gave him a coin.

'We could have had half a baptism for that,' said his wife. 'Look –'

Bibitkin moved on down the line. Suddenly some monks rushed up.

'Come on!' they said. 'That's enough. You get out of here!'

'Get out of here?' cried Bibitkin. 'A man of God in what is supposed to be a place of God?'

'Out you go!'

Bibitkin began to struggle.

'Have you no respect? Have you no respect for a man of God?'

'We've no respect for a person like you,' said one of the monks, and tried to force him away.

Bibitkin was a big, powerful man, however, and broke loose.

'Bastards!' he shouted.

'Come on, come on!'

'I defy you! You look down on Bibitkin because he's just an ordinary village priest, because he shares his bread with the ordinary people. Well, let me tell you, I'd rather share my bread with them, go hungry with them, than sit inside with you!'

'That'll do. Come on, now!'

'I defy you! I defy all you people who live on the fat of the land while the poor go hungry!'

'Come on –'

'They give us cabbage soup,' he shouted to the queue, 'but do you think that's what they're dining off themselves?'

The monks seized him again and forced his arms up behind his back.

'Bastards!'

'Come on, come on!'

'Bastards, your time is coming!'

'You're a disgrace!'

'Oh, Bibitkin's a disgrace, is he? Well, he's not such a disgrace as some who sit inside in the warmth and comfort while out in the fields the children are starving!'

His words began to strike a sympathetic chord in the queue. There were murmurs of approval.

'The children!' cried Bibitkin in apparent agony. 'Oh, the children!'

Suddenly he broke away from the monks. He rushed back up the queue to the couple with the baby and threw himself on his knees before them.

'You think Bibitkin doesn't care!' he shouted. 'You think he cares only about money. But he doesn't, he doesn't! He cares about the children. Here, take your money!'

He fumbled beneath his girdle and threw a handful of coins on to the ground.

'He's drunk!' said someone, amazed.

'The little ones, oh, the little ones!' wept Bibitkin.

The monks tried to pull him to his feet.

'Oh, the little ones! They'll never know Opona. You will know it, brothers, and I will know it, but they won't!'

The monks dragged him upright.

'And you won't know it, either!' he shouted at them angrily. 'Because you won't be here. You'll be swept away. Along with all the others, the rich men, the merchants, the hoarders of grain. Because Opona isn't for the likes of you. It's for the poor and hungry. Oh, when the One-Legged Lady gets here, there'll be a day of reckoning! There will be a day of fire! There will be a weeping and wailing and a gnashing of teeth! The mighty will be cast from their seats and the meek and lowly shall inherit the earth!'

'Come on, now –'

Bibitkin tore himself loose.

'For she's coming, brothers, she's coming!' he cried, raising his eyes ecstatically heavenwards. 'She's on the way! I can feel her hot breath –'

Two men stepped out of the crowd and took him by the arms. One of them Dmitri recognised as the driver of the log-cart. The other was Father Sergei's cousin.

'Come on, now,' they said to Bibitkin, 'you've said enough.'

11

Volkov returned in high good humour.

'Well, that's that,' he said to Dmitri. 'We're ready now.'

'Ready?' said Dmitri. 'For what?'

'For the next march. We'll have spies out and the Cossacks standing by. We'll wait until the various bands have come together – they come from different villages, you see – and then when they're all together and on the march, we'll hit them. We've even got the spot worked out. There's tree cover for the Cossacks and they'll be able to charge downhill. And then it flattens out so they'll be able to harry them. Harrying,' said Volkov, 'is very important. It makes them feel we're right on top of them. That's a good way for rebels to feel.'

'Suppose the march is peaceful?'

Volkov shrugged.

'Is any march peaceful? It doesn't look peaceful, not to the people of Tula, at any rate. It's a show of force. Now there can be only one force in Russia: ours.'

'They're just starving people,' protested Dmitri. 'Do you need to put them down?'

'Yes,' said Volkov. 'Starving people are desperate people, and desperate people make the most intransigent rebels.'

'But starving,' said Dmitri.

'Which is worse?' asked Volkov. 'Starvation or rebellion? I will tell you: rebellion. Rebellion, because its implications go wider. It challenges order, it threatens the State. Whereas starvation, well, it's just starvation. Keep starvation as starvation and you have a simple problem; it's when it becomes rebellion that things get difficult. So,' said Volkov, 'I intend to make sure this stays as starvation.'

'It's unnecessary,' said Dmitri.

'No,' said Volkov, 'I don't think so. Let me tell you about something that happened to me once when I was a young man. At that time I was serving with the army in Uzbekistan. Well, there was trouble there, unrest, I can't remember for what reason. A crowd demonstrated outside the Governor's gates. Well, he was weak, he listened to them. He gave them what they asked for and they went away. But then, do you know what? They came back. The next time something happened, they were there again. And this time they demanded something that he just could not possibly give them. So, well, they rioted and in the end we had to go in. But by this time everyone in the region was involved, so we had to kill far more than we would have needed to if he had been firm in the first place.'

'As a lawyer,' said Dmitri, 'I think justice comes into it.'

'Firmness first,' said Volkov, 'justice after.'

'I don't think you need the Cossacks here,' said Dmitri.

'I had hoped that wouldn't be necessary. I thought they would wait for the Icon. So if we could intercept the Icon – But you haven't found it, have you? And, anyway, they seem to be starting without it.'

'They think it's coming.'

'It had better not,' said Volkov.

He rose to his feet. As he went out of the door, he looked back over his shoulder.

'That girl,' he said: 'I think she should go. Once you break rebels, they run anywhere. They could run there. Go out there and tell her to get back to Kursk. At once.'

Dmitri did not think it at all likely that Ludmilla could be told to do anything, certainly not by him, but the risk was probably real and maybe she ought to be warned. He went off to find the sleigh.

The driver, thinking it would not be needed again that day, had taken it round to the back of the building to park it in one of the sheds. Dmitri found him talking to Bibitkin.

'I feel terrible!' Bibitkin was saying.

He was holding his head in his hands.

'You've just had a drop too much, that's all,' said the driver sympathetically.

'No, no, I *am* terrible. I shouldn't have said what I did. I shouldn't have done what I did. I shouldn't even have been there in the first place. I forgot myself.'

'Well, that's understandable, after all that you'd had to drink,' said the other driver, the driver of the log-cart.

'I went back to my old ways. When I saw that queue there, I forgot. I said to myself, that's my chance. My chance! God forgive me! To try to make money from starving babies!'

He rocked himself to and fro.

'It was shameful.'

'Yes, it was,' said Father Sergei's cousin sternly.

'I know! I know! I see that now,' snuffled Bibitkin. 'I've let everyone down. I've let myself down. I've let *her* down!'

'Her? Your mother-in-law, you mean?'

'Mother-in-law?' Bibitkin raised his head. 'That old bitch! She'll be the first to go if I have my way. And the second will be that pasty-faced, mean-minded brother-in-law of mine! No, the One-Legged Lady. What will she think of me? What will she say to me when she gets here?'

'She'll say you bloody talk too much,' said the log-cart driver, hustling him away.

As Dmitri had feared, Ludmilla proved obdurate.

'No, I'm not going,' she said. 'I'm just beginning to achieve things here.'

'You could buy ahead. Enough to keep them going while you're gone.'

'It's not that. I've been talking to the Zemstvo. It's a case of setting up a system. They're getting in quite a lot of food now but the problem is to distribute it. Well, I can help there, at least as far as Yabloki Sad is concerned.'

'Surely the *Starosta* could handle that?'

'He has a part to play, certainly. He knows people's needs and has a pretty good idea about how best to share it out. I realize now that it's best to leave all that side to him. When I first arrived I just went round all the houses giving something out to everybody. But he knows where there are old people or sick people or where the man of the house would sell it for drink. So I leave all that to him. Someone's got to keep an eye on him, of course, but the women do that very well. No, I find I'm of most use in getting food to the village, the organization side of things. They are not strong,' said Ludmilla, 'on organization.'

'Isn't distribution the responsibility of the Zemstvo?'

'We-e-ell . . .'

Dmitri deduced that the Zemstvo was not strong on organization either. That he could well believe. Any organization in which Uncle Vlady played a prominent part was unlikely to be in the forefront of drive and efficiency. That was the trouble with Russia. Wherever a major problem like famine cropped up, what bodies were there available, especially out in the provinces, to deal with it? The Governor? But the Government was more interested in keeping trouble down than in solving problems. The new Zemstvos? We-e-ll, as Ludmilla had said. The monasteries? Over the past month Dmitri had gained a certain respect for them, but they were hardly the way to solve the social problems of the late nineteenth century.

That left the initiative of individuals: Sonya at Kursk, and Ludmilla up here. When Sonya and her friends had first got together, Dmitri had been inclined to dismiss their efforts as ridiculous amateurism. But, damn it, something had happened. Food, or, at any rate, money had been got and transferred up here to where it was needed. And Ludmilla, at least, had got something into the hands of the peasants.

Perhaps that was no surprise. Almost anything would be better than the lumbering attempts of the creaking, bureaucratic Tsarist State. But it was no way to run a world.

Dmitri knew what was wrong with the running of the world; it was the people who were running it. Basically, they weren't him. They didn't bring to it youth and efficiency and modern ideas. Dmitri had plenty of ideas; but he sometimes suspected uneasily, as on the present occasion, that his own contribution to sorting out the world remained rather too much at the general level. Sonya and Ludmilla, although their grasp of modern ideas was unquestionably weaker, were at least getting something done.

He felt, then, somewhat at a disadvantage in this conversation with Ludmilla. It was all very well for Volkov to say: tell her to go. He hadn't been very successful when he had told her himself, and Dmitri had an uneasy feeling that if he tried he might be even less successful. It was, indeed, far more probable that she would tell him to go.

But there remained the undeniable danger.

'I don't like the thought of your being here alone,' he said. 'Volkov thinks there could be riots and that some of the rioters could come here.'

Ludmilla considered.

'But I don't have to be alone,' she said. 'You could come here.'

This thought had not occurred to Dmitri. But there were things to be said for it.

'We could get to know each other better,' pursued Ludmilla.

Indeed. True, there were those in Kursk who would not think it proper for a young man to spend nights alone in a house with a young girl, but then, Dmitri was someone of modern ideas.

So, it appeared, was Ludmilla.

On returning to the Kaminski Monastery, the first person Dmitri saw, to his surprise, was Father Sergei.

'Just visiting my relatives,' he said, 'to exchange Easter greetings. I'll be back at Kursk in time for the Friday services.'

Volkov, it transpired, had seen him too.

'Yes,' he said to Dmitri. 'I admit, it was a surprise. He'll be going out to his village, I presume?'

'He's going to visit his relatives.'

'Well, yes,' said Volkov.

He did not seem unduly concerned. Dmitri did not quite know how to put it.

'That's all right, is it?'

'Oh, yes.' Volkov smiled. 'I expected the leaders to gather.'

'You don't want –' Dmitri hesitated – 'to do something about it?'

'Beforehand, you mean? No, I don't think so. It's better to let things come to a head. Now that they've got so far. The Cossacks are in position. All we're waiting for now is for them to show themselves. The leaders especially. The more they can be identified with the march, the better. And with what happens afterwards.'

'Father Sergei?' said the monk in the gate-house. 'You've just missed him. I saw him setting out only a few moments ago.'

'For Zapolonye?'

'Yes. To visit his relatives.'

'Does he come here often?'

'Hardly ever. But he wants to exchange Easter greetings. Nice, don't you think, after all these years?'

'He could have brought Father Osip's letters for him.'

'So he could. Just didn't think of it, I suppose.'

'Father Sergei was at this Monastery once, I believe. Was Father Osip here then, too?'

'Oh, yes. They came on almost the same day.'

'And left it together? For Kursk?'

'They were great friends.'

'Allies?' said Dmitri.

'Allies?' The monk looked at him in surprise.

'I gather there was something of a battle about the time that Father Sergei left.'

'Well, yes.' The monk chuckled. 'You could say that. A bit of a hot-head was our Sergei! Mind you, I'm not saying that he was altogether wrong. The Kaminski could have done with a shaking up.' He laid a finger to his lips. 'Still could!'

Dmitri wondered what had been in the bag.

'Well, yes,' said the Father Superior, 'I suppose the time has come for a decision.'

'So what will it be?' asked Dmitri. 'Will you let them take the One-Legged Lady out and carry her through the fields?'

'I still think it's barbarous. But, in the circumstances – if they think it will help them –'

'I would strongly recommend against it,' said Volkov. 'In the circumstances.'

'You would?'

The Father Superior seemed surprised.

'Most definitely.'

The Father Superior shrugged.

'Well, I suppose, in that case –'

'Don't like it.'

The peasants had gathered again in the yard, not as many of them as before, because this was short notice, but still an impressive gathering. As before, the *Starosta* of the village of Zapolonye was their spokesman.

'Well, that's my decision,' said the Father Superior. 'Carrying an icon around the fields is one thing; carrying a body is quite another.'

'Yes, but the Icon's not here.'

'You could carry another.'

'It wouldn't be the same thing.'

'It's the One-Legged Lady,' said someone in the crowd. 'It's got to be the One-Legged Lady.'

'Well, I'm sorry. But she's got to stay in the Monastery.'

'Was she asked about this?' called out someone.

'Asked?' said the Father Superior.

'Yes. You know, did you mention it to her?'

'No,' said the Father Superior.

'Well, I reckon you ought to have done.'

'What sort of answer would you expect me to get?'

'Well, I don't know. You're the expert.'

'She might have sort of winked,' suggested someone.

'She hasn't winked yet,' said the Father Superior. 'At least, not in my experience.'

'Yes, but this is an emergency. You wouldn't expect her to be winking all the time. She's probably tired after all her labours. But on a special occasion like this it might be different.'

'You ought to have asked her,' said the peasants doggedly.

'All right then,' said the Father Superior, 'I will ask her. But if she says no, or, what is more likely, if she doesn't say

146

anything at all, that's it, you understand? She stays here, inside the Monastery. It's not right for her to go gallivanting around at her age.'

They all, Dmitri, too, at the back, followed him to the crypt. It was too crowded for most of them to be able to get down but, looking through the trap-door, Dmitri saw the Father Superior approach the coffin.

'All right, Varvara Morozova, now you listen to me: are you willing to be taken out of the Monastery and carried round the fields?'

Everyone waited.

'No?' said the Father Superior.

'It's a bit special, Varvara,' pleaded one of the peasants. 'We're starving!'

'We know how you feel, Varvara,' said another of the peasants. 'You probably reckon you've done your bit already. We wouldn't disturb you in the ordinary way of things. But the fact is, Varvara, we're in a bad way.'

'It's just the once, Varvara! We won't trouble you again.'

'Wink if you're willing!' instructed the Father Superior.

'Varvara –!'

'Come on, now, love! We'll carry you carefully.'

'No?' said the Father Superior.

'Wait a minute –!'

'No?' he said again. 'No. That's definite. She doesn't want to come.'

The peasants climbed back up out of the crypt.

'He ought to have asked her more politely,' one of them grumbled. 'That was it!'

'She never was one to be bossed around. Who does he bloody think he is, she was probably thinking? "Wink?" Who the hell does he think he's talking to?'

'We should have asked her ourselves. She never did have any time for the likes of him.'

'The fact is, she was probably pissed off with him.'

They went unhappily away.

Last of all, the Father Superior came up. He shut the trap-door firmly behind him.

'You know,' he said to Dmitri, 'for a moment I thought –'

'That would have been too like the Queen of Spades,' said Dmitri. He went out into the yard. The peasants were huddled together, talking.

'Well, it's unfortunate, that's what I say.'

'It is. What are we going to do?'

'It doesn't leave us much choice, does it?'

Ludmilla had sent her sleigh for him. It had called in first at the town to pick up provisions and now, as it came in through the gates, Ivan, who had been sent to gather them, was sitting uneasily among the purchases. He made space for Dmitri and the sleigh set off again, this time for Yabloki Sad.

They sat there for some time in silence. There seemed something constrained about Ivan's manner. He kept looking at Dmitri.

At last he spoke.

'I can't figure you out,' he said. 'One moment you're thick with him, the next moment you're in with her. You can't be both. They're not on the same side. Whose side are you on?'

It was the question one was always asking in Russia; and one which Dmitri was finding increasingly difficult to answer.

Ludmilla's house was a large, wooden, single-storey building surrounded by lawns which dropped down to a river. A verandah ran along the front and French windows opened on to the rear. An ornamental fret-work hung down from a rustic porch protecting the door and continued round the house under the eaves. It was the kind of house that Dmitri's difficult grandfather lived in; who might, had he been here, have been giving his grandson some straight looks just at the moment.

Ludmilla, whose parents might also have been eyeing her askance, was stretched on the sofa beside Dmitri. Escaping from them, she was beginning to understand, had been one of the points of her sortie to the north, and she was relishing both her independence and the new feeling of being mistress of all she surveyed, certainly of the house and almost, she felt, equally certainly of Dmitri.

'Your great-grandmother, then?' he was saying.

'Yes. Or was it great-great?' Anyway, the One-Legged Lady.'

'A remarkable woman!'

'The female line has been in decline ever since,' said Ludmilla sadly.

'She obviously felt very passionately about things,' said Dmitri.

'Yes,' said Ludmilla, who thought that in that respect the line was possibly reviving.

'And she gave all her money away?'

'I think most of it had gone already,' said Ludmilla, 'during the dissipated part of her career.'

'It's nice to know it wasn't wasted,' said Dmitri. 'Now in my family the money's just leaked away without anyone doing anything special with it. Except use it to quarrel with anyone who fancied themself their superior: like the Tsar. The result is there isn't any money in the family now and I've got to go out to work.'

'I wish I could go out to work,' sighed Ludmilla.

'Ah, well, there you are! The woman question –'

But Ludmilla was not interested in the general. She had particular things in mind; and, shortly afterwards, so had Dmitri.

They heard someone come into the house. Ludmilla sat up.

'Korol? Is that you?'

She went to the door.

'Oh, hello, Ivan. Put it there, will you? Now, what am I going to do with it, Ivan? It's seed corn,' she explained to Dmitri, 'for their fields. The thing is, we want them to plant it, not eat it.'

'Keep it,' said Ivan. 'Then, one spring day, go down to the fields with them. Give it them then and stand over them while they plant it. I'll tell you the day.'

Ludmilla nodded.

'Right,' she said, 'put it in the cellar for now, will you? And bring me the keys. What about the other stuff?'

'The *Starosta*'s here.'

'Very well, I'll watch him divide it out.'

They went out into the yard. The *Starosta* was there with several men. At a word from Ludmilla, the men began to unload the sleigh. As they unloaded the *Starosta* divided everything out into separate portions. When he had finished, the men picked up the portions. Ludmilla and the *Starosta* went with them into the village. They started calling in at each house.

Dmitri had gone with them. As he was standing in the street he saw a man come out of one of the houses.

'Who's that?' he asked Ludmilla.

'That? Oh, that's Korol. He works for Marputin.'

'What's he doing here?'

'Well, you remember that I had got Marputin to agree an advance to each household against the purchase price of each house if they sold? He's arranging it.'

'And he works for Marputin?'

'He's Marputin's man.'

'I think I would like a word with him.'

He was an odd sort of man to find in a peasant village. He wasn't a peasant at all but quite definitely a man of the town. Almost a Barin, you might say. Very neatly dressed, almost too well dressed. Not quite a Barin, though, on second thoughts. What was it that Avdotya Feodorovna had said? More like someone who worked in one of the big St Petersburg department stores. Except for his hands. Not soft, St Petersburg hands but rough, craftsman's hands. A restorer, perhaps, thought Dmitri. A restorer of icons.

'Kameron,' said Dmitri, 'Assistant Procurator. I'm investigating the theft of an icon. From the monastery at Kursk.'

'Kursk?' said the man.

'Yes. I think you know the icon I mean?'

'Do I?' said the man.

'You should. You spent a long time looking at it. That was before your unfortunate accident with the cart.'

'Oh, yes,' said the man, 'I remember the accident. But I saw a lot of icons that day.'

'Including the One-Legged Lady.'

'The One-Legged Lady? Of course. But I didn't spend a lot of time on her.'

'Enough,' said Dmitri.

'Enough for what?'

'To work out how it would have to be done.'

'I don't follow you,' said the man.

'Or did you leave it to them? After you'd made up your mind that you wanted it?'

'I don't understand you.'

'That's your job, isn't it? Going round looking for icons. For Marputin's collection.'

'I have a general interest in icons, certainly –'

'More than general. You buy them.'

'Well, now –'

'The one you bought from Bibitkin, for example.'

'That was an exception –'

'You tried to buy others. I have the names of the people.'

The man gave a forced laugh.

'Well, is there anything wrong with that?'

'No. Not if you confine your interest to buying them.'

'Well, then –'

'But did you?'

'If I did work for Marputin,' said the man, 'he wouldn't want to have anything to do with anything that was illegal.'

'Was that why you had to give the icon back to Bibitkin?'

'No,' said the man, 'not really. We saw that it was getting him into trouble, that was all.'

'And arousing too much interest?'

'It was, I admit, not strictly within the bounds of the law. The icon wasn't his to sell. I was tempted by it, I must confess. It was a nice icon. And I shouldn't have made the offer. When I had had a chance to think about it afterwards, I realised that of course it wouldn't do. So I handed it back.'

'And the One-Legged Lady?'

'Nothing to do with me.'

The man hesitated.

'All right, I admit I thought about it. It was such a – well, you know, you don't often see something like that. It's by

151

the Master of Tomsk. One of the only three pieces of his that survived. But it wouldn't be right for a private collection, it's too big. Oh, I know some people can take big pieces, but you've got to see it in the light of the rest of the collection. It wouldn't do. All right. I did think about it, I even mentioned it to Marputin. But he said no.'

'But you came and looked at it.'

'That was before.'

'Checking it out?'

'Only to see if it was a possible. When I thought about it afterwards, I realised it wasn't.'

'But you spoke to Marputin about it.'

'Yes.'

'Why was that? If you'd already made up your mind?'

The man hesitated.

'I had an offer.'

'An offer?'

'Yes. Somebody offered it to me.'

'Was this before it was stolen or after?'

'After. That's what made me go Marputin. I thought, if it was stolen already – well, you know, there's a kind of illicit market in these things, and once an object is on the market, well, it doesn't seem quite the same –'

'So there was a chance Marputin might take it?'

'A chance, yes. But he didn't.'

'Would you care to tell me who it was who made you the offer?'

'No, I wouldn't.'

'It would substantiate your story.'

'I didn't steal the Icon,' said the man quietly, 'and you couldn't show that I did.'

'Do you know where it is now?'

'No.'

'Or if it is moving?'

'Moving?' said the man.

'Yes. Here. Like you.'

12

Ivan came into the house.

'I think you should stay inside today,' he said to Ludmilla.

Ludmilla was surprised. He spoke very seriously and without his usual apologetic deference.

'Oh, why?' she said.

'They are going to march.'

'March?'

'On Tula. To demand food.'

'But why should I stay inside? Oughtn't I to be going with them?'

'No,' said Ivan.

'No,' said Dmitri.

She turned and looked at him.

'But why not?'

'Because they're demanding it, not asking it.'

'I don't understand.'

'There will be violence.'

'But –'

'The Barin's right,' Ivan cut in. 'It's not the place for you.'

'Perhaps if I am there, I will be able to prevent it.'

'You stay out of it,' said Dmitri.

A little angry spot appeared in each of Ludmilla's cheeks.

'I certainly will not stay out of it,' she said sharply, 'not if there's a chance that I might be able to do something.'

'That's exactly it,' said Dmitri. 'You won't be able to do anything.'

'I am not so sure of that,' said Ludmilla crisply.

Ivan looked to Dmitri in appeal.

'Ivan is concerned for your safety.'

Ludmilla shrugged.

'They're marching on Tula,' she said, 'not on me.'

'It's not just them. There will be Cossacks waiting.'

'Cossacks?' said Ivan.

'Cossacks?' said Ludmilla.

'Volkov has made plans.'

'They will be walking into a trap? Then someone must warn them!' cried Ludmilla.

Zapolonye, empty before, was full of people now. Burly peasants in their worn winter coats and their heavy boots crowded the single street. Many of them were carrying sticks.

Several of them looked curiously at Ludmilla.

'Who's she?'

'She's our lady,' said someone from Yabloki Sad.

'What's she doing here?'

Ludmilla began to push her way through the crowd.

At the front some men were trying to organize the peasants into rows. Dmitri recognised one of them. It was the man who had been so hostile the other day. Lev. His eyes widened when he saw Ludmilla.

'Who's she?'

'She's our lady.'

'What do you mean, our lady?'

'The One-Legged Lady.'

'She's not the One-Legged Lady!'

'She is, more or less!'

'She isn't. We can't have her here.'

'She might bring us luck, Lev.'

'We don't *need* luck,' said Lev.

'Oh, yes, you do,' said Ludmilla.

'You keep out of it,' said Lev.

Ludmilla turned and faced the crowd.

'You need luck,' she said, 'because you'll be walking into a trap. They know you're coming and they've got the Cossacks waiting for you.'

'Cossacks!'

'Don't listen to her,' said Lev. 'It's all nonsense.'

'No, it's not,' said Dmitri.

'Who the hell is he?'

'It's that Barin who was here the other day!'

'Well, he can bloody get out again, can't he?'

'When I saw him, he was with the Corps of Gendarmes!'

'The Gendarmes!'

They began to move in on Dmitri.

'Now, look here, brothers –' began Ivan.

'We know whose side you're on, Ivan!' said Lev spitefully.

'No, you don't,' said Ivan. 'You listen to him. He's right about the Cossacks.'

'I was with Volkov the other day,' said Dmitri, 'and that's how I know. He told me the Cossacks were moving into position.

'We're wasting time,' said Lev. 'Let's get on with it.'

'No, wait a minute.'

It was the village *Starosta*, the grey-haired man who had been the spokesman for the peasants in the exchanges with the Father Superior.

'Let's hear more of this. The Cossacks are already there, are they?'

'Yes. They're waiting for you to get together with the other groups and then they'll start.'

'We'll be too many for them,' said Lev.

'They'll carve you into little pieces,' said Dmitri.

The peasants looked doubtfully at one another.

'Come on!' said Lev impatiently.

'No, wait!' said the *Starosta*. 'We need to do a bit of thinking.'

'We've done our thinking,' said Lev.

'Thinking doesn't get you a full stomach,' said a man standing beside him.

'No,' said the *Starosta*, 'but it might save you from getting killed.'

'Hear Panteleimon's words!' said a new voice. It was the *Starosta* from Yabloki Sad.

That seemed the general opinion.

'Make them short,' said Lev unwillingly.

'It goes back to what we were saying earlier,' said the *Starosta*. 'Do we march in peace or in war?'

'We've decided that!' said Lev.

'Yes. And we decided for peace. But now, suddenly, it's become war.'

'That wasn't our fault,' said someone.

'We would have marched for peace. Behind the Old Lady. But that bastard of a Father Superior wouldn't let us have her!'

'So it's got to be war,' said Lev.

'Has it?'

'I'm not afraid of the Cossacks!'

'Well, I bloody am,' said the *Starosta*. 'And so would you be if you'd been on the receiving end of one of their charges, like I have. That Barin's right. They'll cut us to pieces. And what good would that do us? What good would it do our wives and children if they've got no man to work for them?'

'We've had this talk!' said Lev.

'And we decided rightly. And what I say is, we should stick to our decision.'

'Are we going to do nothing?' said Lev. 'Stay at home while our children starve?'

'No, I didn't say that, I said the question was whether we marched in peace or in war. We decided for peace and I say we should stick with that. March in war and the Cossacks will have their day. Go in peace and they won't be able to touch us.'

'I wish I could believe that, Panteleimon,' objected the *Starosta* of Yabloki Sad uneasily, 'but I don't think it will matter much to them whether we're marching in peace or in war. The fact that we're marching will be enough.'

'And how would they know we were marching in peace?' asked someone.

'When we talked about it before,' said Panteleimon, 'it was agreed that we would show our peaceful intentions by carrying a holy emblem in front of us. The Old Lady Icon would have been best but that's gone to Kursk and anyway someone has stolen it. So we agreed we'd settle on the Old Lady herself.'

'Yes, but now she can't come, Panteleimon.'

'She can't. But someone else can.' He looked at Ludmilla. 'Someone who's nearly as good.'

'You're not suggesting they march behind her!' said Dmitri.

'Why not?' said the starosta. He turned to Ludmilla. 'You'd be willing, wouldn't you? To show we meant peace?'

'Yes,' said Ludmilla.

Someone came bursting through the crowd.

'It's crazy! It's crazy!' he was shouting. 'Why can't you wait? She's on her way, I tell you! On her way! She could be here in a couple of days if you wanted!'

It was Bibitkin.

'Him again!'

He rushed up to Panteleimon.

'Why can't you wait? She's on her way! The One-Legged Lady!'

'Yes, yes. So you say.'

'Two days! She could be here in two days!'

'Yes, yes, I know. But look, we're here now, aren't we? We can't wait.'

'But she'll be here! She'll be here! I promise!'

'Yes, yes.'

He was hustled away. The peasants began to form up into ranks.

Bibitkin went over to one of the houses and stood against the wall watching despairingly.

Dmitri made his way round to him.

'What was that you said?'

'She could be here,' moaned Bibitkin. 'If only you would wait!'

'How do you know?'

Bibitkin suddenly saw who it was and froze.

Dmitri pushed him back against the wall.

'How do you know she will be here?'

'I – I –'

'You know where she is, don't you?'

He took Bibitkin by the collar and shook him.

'What are you doing up here? Are you offering it to them? Like you offered it to Marputin?'

'No, no. This is different!'

'How is it different?'

'We – we don't want money.'

Dmitri shook him contemptuously.

'You expect me to believe that?'

'It's true! It's true!'

'You're offering it them out of the goodness of your hearts?'

'Yes!' said Bibitkin defiantly.

Dmitri released him.

Someone was calling out orders at the front. The crowd was getting ready to march.

'Why won't they take it?'

'They don't believe me. They think it's just drink talking. But it isn't, it isn't!'

'No,' said Dmitri, 'it isn't.'

The procession set off, Ludmilla, the two *Starostas* and Lev walking at the head, the others forming a column about eight abreast behind. Dmitri slipped into one of the rear ranks. What he was hoping to do he wasn't quite sure. Something. At least if he was there he might be able to do something.

Once he caught sight of Ludmilla. She was pale but determined. That was the note of the whole thing: determined. There was not much animation. Occasionally someone struck up a song, sometimes a hymn. Usually, however, the men marched in silence.

Dmitri realized suddenly that, weakened as they were by hunger, it was all they could do to keep going. They had no breath to spare for singing or even talk.

At first the day was dark. There was no light coming through the clouds and the woods were dark against the snow. After a while, however, the clouds lifted and the sun came out, making the crystals sparkle as they had done on the day when he had first driven out to the Monastery at Kursk.

They had been tramping for some hours when ahead of him he saw a hill with a few fir trees on top. At first he thought it was trees all over, since the lower slopes were dark. Gradually he realized that they were dark with people, the same black smudge that he had seen at the gates of the monasteries, only this time much larger. Occasionally something flashed in the darkness. When he got nearer he saw that many in the crowd were carrying icons.

His party marched wearily up to the hill and then joined the others sitting in the snow. A small group of men came down the slope towards them. The starostas went forward to meet them. When they came closer, Dmitri recognized two of the men: Father Sergei and his cousin.

So Volkov had been right, thought Dmitri dully: the leaders had arrived.

When Father Sergei saw Ludmilla, he stopped, astonished.

'What are you doing here, Miss Mitkin?'

'I am here as a pledge,' she said, 'that the intention of the march is peaceful.'

'Well, yes, but –'

He seemed, not unnaturally, taken aback. Then he recovered.

'Miss Mitkin,' he said, 'the intention behind the march *is* peaceful. That is why I am here. It might have been otherwise. But now the matter is resolved. It will be peaceful. There is always a risk, however, that something could go wrong. Miss Mitkin, it would be better if you left.'

'How will they know your intention is peaceful?' she said.

'How will they –?'

Dmitri realized suddenly that Father Sergei did not know about the Cossacks. Ludmilla realized it at the same moment.

'Father Sergei,' she said, 'not far away from here are Cossacks. They intend to attack.'

'Cossacks! Are you sure?'

'Yes,' said Dmitri, stepping forward.

'Dmitri Alexandrovich!'

'I have spoken to Volkov. He has made preparations.'

'But Cossacks!'

'He feared that the march might get out of hand.'

'There was a danger of that, but –'

He shook his head.

'Cossacks! Why do they do this to us? It's a peaceful demonstration. By starving people!'

'It might not have been. The thing is, however, that they are already in position. They are waiting only for you all to come together and then they will strike. Unless –'

Once they had got to the top of the hill he could see the Cossacks. There was a smaller hill some way away covered with trees and in among the trees men in uniform were moving. He caught the glint of blades and perhaps of rifles.

He walked down the hill towards them, Ludmilla beside him, and then the two *Starostas*, with Father Sergei carrying an icon. Woman and icon; Dmitri had no great confidence either that the Cossacks were chivalrous or that they were religious but it might make them pause.

His feet floundered in the snow. There was no track here, just the deep snow, deeper, as they discovered in some places than in others. Neither Dmitri nor Ludmilla were used to walking. The two *Starostas*, however, stepped forward with the slow, patient stride of peasants; and Father Sergei, Dmitri noticed, after a while fell comfortably into step with them.

They had reached the bottom of the hill now and were wading through deep drifts. On the slopes of the hill opposite them they could see quite clearly the men and horses waiting.

An officer rode down the slope to meet them.

'Well?' he said, looking at them curiously, however.

'Kameron,' said Dmitri, stepping forward. 'Assistant Procurator, city of Kursk. This is Miss Mitkin, daughter of the Governor.'

He did not bother to introduce the others. The officer could see who they were; and it would not make much difference.

'What are you doing here?'

'We have been satisfying ourselves that the gathering is a peaceful one.'

'Peaceful?' said the officer, looking back towards the hill behind them.

'Yes. The *Starostas* of the villages concerned invited us, me as a representative of the law, Miss Mitkin as a reputable independent witness, to satisfy ourselves in that respect. We have done so and that is what we will testify at the inquiry.'

'Inquiry?'

'The public inquiry that will follow should there be a confrontation.'

The officer hesitated, then swung his horse round and rode back up the hill. Dmitri doubted whether the concepts of 'public', 'inquiry' or, indeed, 'law' meant much to them – the Cossacks' allegiance was personal and to the Tsar only – but the formal terms might insert a wedge of doubt into what was otherwise a wall of unquestioning certainty.

The officer was riding back again, this time with a group of other officers, two of them senior.

'What is this?' said one of them harshly.

'Kameron,' repeated Dmitri, 'Assistant Procurator, City of Kursk. Miss Mitkin, daughter of the Governor.'

'What are you doing here?'

'Satisfying ourselves as to the peaceful intentions of the people gathered here.'

'What's it got to do with you?'

'We have been asked to attend as formal witnesses.'

'Witnesses?'

'There will naturally be an inquiry should this end in a confrontation,' said Dmitri, 'and very possibly a trial.'

'We don't try rebels,' said one of the senior officers.

'I wasn't thinking of them,' said Dmitri.

The man urged his horse forwards until he was alongside Dmitri looking down on him.

'If there is a trial,' he said threateningly, 'it would be of people consorting with rebels.'

'An officer of law?' said Dmitri. 'A lady from one of the most reputable families in the province?'

'Let's not waste time,' said one of the other officers.

'What shall we do with them?'

'Get them out of the way. Until it's all over.'

'The people over there are just hungry people,' said Father Sergei. 'Have you no feeling?'

The officer rode over to him.

'Another rebel?' he said. 'Well, we know what to do about you, too.'

'Do you know what to do about God?' said Father Sergei. He raised the icon and shook it.

'Law, Society and Church,' said Dmitri. 'Do you think you can ignore all three and hope to get away with it?'

One of the younger officers came up to Dmitri and looked hard at him.

'I know this man,' he said. 'He was with Volkov.'

'With Volkov?'

'That's right,' said Dmitri. 'I work with him.'

The senior officers looked puzzled.

'I don't understand that,' one of them said.

'Well, you ought to,' said Dmitri. 'I have been trying to see if a peaceful resolution is possible; he has been making arrangements in case it is not.'

The senior officers nodded. They looked at each other and then rode a little way away and conferred. Then they came riding back.

'All right,' they said. 'We'll let them disperse peacefully.'

'What about the procession?' asked Father Sergei.

'We said we'd let them disperse,' said one of the senior officers. 'That's all.'

'It's just to draw attention to their plight,' said Father Sergei.

The officer shook his head.

'Can't have that,' he said. 'It's provocative.'

'Will they disperse, do you think?' Dmitri asked Father Sergei.

Father Sergei hesitated.

'Hunger bites deep,' he said. 'Now that they've got here, they'll want to see something for it.'

'Can they be given assurances?' Dmitri asked the officers. 'Like what?'

'That an effort will be made to get food to them.'

The Cossacks shook their heads.

'Nothing to do with us,' they said.

'Is there someone around?' asked Dmitri. 'Someone they could talk to?'

'There's only us.'

'And it's not much good talking to us,' said the other senior officer, with a little, hard smile. 'We have orders; all we do is carry them out.'

'You'll attack?'

'If they don't disperse, yes.'

Dmitri looked at the *Starostas*.

'Could you persuade them?'

'We could try,' said Simeon.

'They'll want something,' said Panteleimon, shaking his head.

Both sides, the Cossacks and the peasants, stood there waiting, looking at Dmitri. He couldn't think what else he could try.

'Perhaps that will persuade them, said Ludmilla bitterly.

She pointed through the trees to where the head of a long column was just coming into view.

'We haven't asked for reinforcements,' said one of the senior officers, surprised.

'Those aren't reinforcements,' said the other senior officer.

'Then what –?'

Perched among the parcels in the leading cart, like Father Christmas, was a figure Dmitri recognised: Uncle Vlady.

13

'You can't fob us off with this!' cried Lev.

'It's all right as it is,' said Panteleimon more neutrally, 'but it won't keep us going for more than a week!'

'A fortnight,' said the doctor – one of Vera's friends – who had come with the convoy. 'After that we'll be round again. The aim is to set up a system.'

'System?' said Dmitri suspiciously. The one thing he knew about systems in Russia was that they did not work.

'Yes. The problem now is not getting the food in but getting it out. We've got plenty coming in. You'd be amazed at the public response. Places like Kursk . . . Why, only yesterday they sent us a banker's order that was positively huge. There's an absolutely wonderful Procurator working for them down there, I believe . . . with that sort of money, there's going to be no shortage of food.'

'But how are you going to get it out?' asked Ludmilla.

'Well, that's the problem. It always is in Russia. Plenty of enthusiasm at the start but no consistent drive afterwards to carry it through. The truth is, we're short of the right people. But we'll get there, we'll get there.'

'Want some help?' said Ludmilla.

The peasants had possibly even less confidence in official systems than Dmitri did, but in people they could believe; especially around Yabloki Sad. When it was agreed that Ludmilla would coordinate all the supplies in that area, the two *Starostas* and Father Sergei had no difficulty in swinging those peasants behind her. That left, of course, the rest of the villages around Tula; but Father Sergei did sterling work in persuading the peasants that if the Zemstvo could get food out here while the snow was still deep on the ground, then they would probably be able to manage it throughout the summer until the next harvest. It is true that the peasants were still not at all clear about what the Zemstvo was. However, their hazy perception of it as something to do with the One-Legged Lady got it off to a good start.

At any rate, to Lev's disgust they went home.

'You came for food and you've got food,' said Dmitri reasonably. 'What do you want: Opona?'

Well, yes, they did want Opona. But they were realistic fellows at heart and suspected that Opona was one of those things that always gets put off.

'Paradoxically,' said the Father Superior, 'it always seems closest when it is furthest away. That is to say, there's most talk of it when things are at their worst, when there is a famine, say. When things get better, somehow the prospect recedes.'

This was back at Kursk and said over the *zakuski*.

'It is an illusion,' declared Volkov, thawed enough to help himself to a second portion of salmon caviar.

That had proved the trickiest part of the whole business: dealing with Volkov. Dmitri had managed it in the end only by pointing out to Volkov that Ludmilla had assumed, in the peasants' eyes, much of the persona of the original One-Legged Lady: and that, faced with this unprecedented emergency, all that he had been able to do was convert – pervert, was the word Dmitri used, which was possibly a mistake – the One-Legged Lady's role from an insurrectionary one to one making for social stability. This he had achieved, as was witnessed by the peasants' peaceful withdrawal.

Volkov had been unable immediately to think of a reply to this one and had stood the Cossacks down. He had remained troubled, however.

'Isn't it just a temporary solution? Aren't the rebellious tendencies still there?'

'Well, yes,' said the Father Superior, over the lemony *solyanka*, 'Opona is always there, inside people.'

'Well, then –'

'You can't have Cossacks standing by all the time,' objected Dmitri.

'Why not?' said Volkov.

Dmitri looked at the Father Superior and the Father Superior looked at Dmitri.

'I don't think the *solyanka* is quite so good,' said the Father Superior. 'Shall we send it back? Try the *rassolnik*, perhaps?'

'I think it may have been one of the *pirozhkis* – something that accompanied it.'

'Maybe it would be better to move on,' said the Father Superior. He contemplated the sturgeon and salmon and roach and the hazel hen, the turkey and blackcock. 'Now, what were we talking about?'

'Famine, I think,' said Dmitri.

'Oh, yes. Well, spiced crane for me. And what about you?' He turned to Volkov. 'Meat balls?'

'The turkey, I think,' said Volkov.

'I agree with you,' said the Father Superior, back to Dmitri. 'In the end, the real issue is the harvest.'

'With the money it's now getting, the Zemstvo will be able to supply them with seed.'

'Let's hope it comes up. And that the weather is right this year.'

'There's not much we can do about that.'

'Well, as a matter of fact ... You know. I have been thinking things over. Why shouldn't we do as they ask? It would be a gesture of reconciliation. One monastery to another. The Church to the people.'

'Give it back?'

'I wasn't thinking of going quite as far as that. Lend it, perhaps. So that it could be carried in their Easter Procession.'

'You're surely not going to let them take it out into the fields?' said Volkov, aghast.

'Why not? It would be restoring ancient custom. Isn't that something that the Corps of Gendarmes would wish to encourage?'

'Well, yes, but –'

'And now that, thanks to Dmitri Alexandrovich, we have the One-Legged Lady back again –'

*   *   *

On their way back from Tula, at Dmitri's request, they had called in at the Monastery at Kursk. Dmitri had gone straight round to Peter Karpov's workshop at the rear of the log shed; where he had been fortunate enough to catch the carpenter in.

'Just back from Tula,' he had said.

'Oh, yes?' said Peter Karpov uneasily.

'Been talking to Bibitkin.'

'Yes?'

Peter Karpov looked even more uneasy.

'Yes. A spot of trouble up there. Nearly.'

'Nearly?' said Peter Karpov.

'Yes. We were able to stop it in time. Thanks partly to Father Sergei. And to Bibitkin.'

'Bibitkin?' whispered Peter Karpov.

'He had done his best you know. But they wouldn't believe him. Or, at least, they hadn't quite got round to believing him when the whole thing blew up. So they hadn't agreed to take her. Even as a gift. I must confess, I'm a little surprised at that,' said Dmitri: 'that you were offering it to them as a gift, I mean. That had not been the original idea, surely? Was it just that you were finding it more difficult to dispose of than you had thought?'

The carpenter moistened his lips.

'You had tried Marputin. Perhaps it was then that you realized it? That it wasn't quite the thing for a private collection. You knew, of course, that he was interested in icons and not too scrupulous about how he acquired them. That dubious purchase from Bibitkin! But you hadn't, perhaps, realised that the One-Legged Lady was different. Too big, for a start. And too well-known. So well-known that it wasn't just the Church that was investigating its loss but also the Procurator's office. Not to mention the Corps of Gendarmes!'

Peter Karpov looked sick.

'Was that when you decided you had to get rid of it? When the Corps of Gendarmes became involved? Get rid of it quick, even if it meant giving it away? Or was it, perhaps, when Marputin's man, Korol, insisted on returning the icon he had bought from Bibitkin and you realized that they were taking care to show that they had no links with you?'

Dmitri stood up and began to prowl around the workshop.

'Talking of links,' he said, 'it was cheeky of you to cut the chains beforehand. And to do it so publicly. At least when Father Kiril could see you. But probably you thought you needn't bother about him.'

He came to the framework that the carpenter had built to make it easier to carry the One-Legged Lady when she was taken out to bless the fields.

'Ah, yes,' he said. 'With this you could manage with three men: yourself, the cart driver, and Bibitkin. Anyone else?'

'No,' whispered the carpenter.

'No. A bit of a struggle, though, and you wanted to make sure you had plenty of time. Which you wouldn't have had if you'd had to cut the chains as well. So you cut them beforehand and resealed them with wax so that no one would notice.'

He came back and stood in front of the carpenter.

'So,' he said, 'all that remains is for you to tell me where you are keeping her.

'You could say she was here all the time,' said Dmitri, – 'I'll have the roach, I think – since she was behind the logs in the log-shed.'

'Fresh from the Caspian,' said the Father Superior. 'Or nearly fresh, since they've been kept in ice.'

'The vodka, too. I hope,' said Dmitri.

'So,' said Father Kiril, 'had enough gadding about, have you? Well, my beauty, I see I'm going to have to keep my eye on you in future.'

'I think the intention is to send her up to Tula,' said Dmitri mildly. 'Just for a week or two.'

'Tula' Father Kiril replied. Then –

'Tula is no place for a lady!' he thundered.

'Funny,' said Dmitri. 'That's exactly what His Excellency said to me.'

It had happened like this.

'We had always hoped that Ludmilla would unite herself to some nice, sensible young man,' cooed the Governor's wife.

'Preferably with some land,' said the Governor.

'Exactly how extensive is the estate at Gorni Platok?' asked the Governor's wife.

Alarm bells rang all over the place.

'I am afraid my grandfather is still in residence,' said Dmitri quickly, 'and he is very eccentric.'

'But surely the house is big enough to accomodate –?'

'The fact is, he can't stand icons.'

'Can't stand icons?'

'Not only will he not allow them into the house, he has said he will disinherit me if I marry into a family with icons in theirs.'

'Oh, dear!' said the Governor.

'Of course,' said Dmitri, 'you could always dispose of them. To Marputin, say –'

'We haven't seen much of Marputin lately,' said the Governor's wife sadly. 'Which is why we thought that perhaps you –'

It was then that the Governor had said it.

'Tula is no place for a young lady,' he said.

'I think,' said Dmitri, 'that Ludmilla will make up her own mind.'

'What?' said Father Kiril.

'I said that the Old Lady will make up her own mind,' said Dmitri.

'Well, that's true enough,' agreed Father Kiril. 'Always has done and always will. Not one of these flighty youngsters. Always down to the fields.'

'Although, from what I hear,' said Dmitri naughtily, 'that wasn't always true.'

Unexpectedly, Father Kiril chuckled.

'That's so,' he agreed.

'Good heavens!' said Dmitri. 'You weren't there yourself when –?'

'No respect!' bawled Father Kiril. 'No respect!'

'What?' said Dmitri.

* * *

169

'Out to the Monastery again? Vera had said when he had told the little circle of friends where he was going for dinner that evening. 'You're really becoming quite an obscurantist, Dmitri!'

Her sharpness had increased since she had learned of Ludmilla's invitation to come up and stay with her – permanently – on the estate at Yabloki Sad. Dmitri had declined on the grounds that it would mean abandoning a promising career.

'We knew you'd put your career first,' said Igor. 'You usually do.'

'Even if it means falling into the arms of the Corps of Gendarmes!' said Vera, who was not at all pleased at his falling into anyone's arms other than hers.

Even the gentle Sonya had been bothered by that.

'The Corps of Gendarmes! You really should be careful, Dmitri, about the people you associate with.'

Advice that was repeated to Dmitri by Volkov himself.

'I'm not saying that you're without talent,' he added. 'It's just that it expresses itself in ways that are not quite – well, not quite ordinary. Now that really is a handicap if you're looking to a good career.'

Not quite ordinary – not even ordinary for Dmitri – was a new enthusiasm he seemed to have developed since his return from Tula. This was for local government. Boris Petrovich, surfing in on the wave of popular feeling created by his efforts on behalf of the starving, was duly elected to the Kursk Zemstvo. Shortly afterwards a by-election came up.

'We need good men,' he said to Dmitri.

Dmitri discussed it with his friends. Vera Samsonova, surprisingly – or, perhaps, not so surprisingly as it became apparent that the Zemstvo Dmitri was contemplating was the Kursk one not the Tula one – was all in favour.

'That's where the future is,' she said, 'for Russia. That's where we need new men.'

'Like Uncle Vlady,' said Sonya.

'Not like Uncle Vlady,' said Dmitri.

He was thinking it over, however.

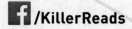 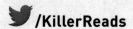

Printed by RR Donnelley at Glasgow, UK